Rally to Kill

RALLY TO KILL

Bill Knox

Constable • London

Constable & Robinson Ltd
3 The Lanchesters
162 Fulham Palace Road
London W6 9ER
www.constablerobinson.com

First published in Great Britain 1975
This edition published in Great Britain by Constable,
an imprint of Constable & Robinson Ltd 2008

A copy of the British Library Cataloguing in Publication
Data is available from the British Library.

UK ISBN: 978-1-84529-862-3

Printed and bound in the EU

Chapter One

'When you're a cop, what you've got to remember is that your average John Citizen may be all for law and order but he'll still feel as uneasy as hell when you land on his doorstep. That's human nature. Some will be either aggressive or on the defensive before you even open your mouth – and that's human nature too. A cop isn't part of their normal life-pattern. You'll worry them, even when they need you.'

Pausing, wishing he could light a cigarette, Detective Chief Inspector Colin Thane, head of Glasgow's Millside Division C.I.D., flicked over to the last page of notes in front of him. Every Divisional chief took a turn as a visiting lecturer at the city's Police Training Centre in Oxford Street, in the very heart of the old, notorious Gorbals. But, as always, he wondered how much of what he'd said over the last forty minutes had really registered with his audience.

Eight men and two girls sat in front of him in the small, brightly lit classroom. Their uniforms were still new enough to show the tailor-shop folds. A few weeks before they'd had different, ordinary lives, but now they were desperately needed rookie police officers in a city that had a chronically undermanned police force – six hundred below strength in an authorized establishment of three thousand two hundred.

Thane sighed to himself. This batch seemed younger than most. Some were almost baby-faced. One of the girls, a slim, good-looking redhead with a nameplate in front of her which said she was Katherine Manson, wore her uniform as if she could have been a fashion model. Next to her, a lanky dark-haired constable identified as Robert Deacon sat stifling a yawn and appeared more interested in the redhead's legs than the rest of his surroundings.

'Right,' said Thane with a touch of despair. 'A couple of final reminders and we'll wrap up this session.' From the doorway at the back, Sergeant Easter, the training course instructor, gave a fractional nod meaning he agreed time was up. 'Each of you will have a different notion about what you'd like to do within this force. For all I know, God help us, one of you may even finish as Chief Constable.'

That drew the usual grins and the lanky probationer nudged the redhead, who gave him a quick scowl. Thane let the chuckles settle, wondering if anyone had told them the statistics involved. One constable in eight could hope to make sergeant during his police career, one sergeant in four should eventually become an inspector, and from there on it became a mixture of luck, ability and how your face fitted.

'On the other hand, some of you may be misguided enough to settle for the detective branch,' Thane continued dryly. 'For you, what I've been trying to say this afternoon starts with never taking anything for granted.

'Somebody may tell you it is raining outside, and it may look that way. So you'll be sensible and take a coat to be prepared – but until you've been out and got wet you've no personal proof. The other aspect is discretion. The liberty and ability to decide what you think fit, either absolutely or within limits. You'll learn

6

discretion the hard way, because even Sergeant Easter can't teach it.'

At the back, Easter gave a grim nod of agreement. A few of the rookies looked puzzled, some faces remained blank, but the lanky youngster named Deacon showed a sudden interest.

'There's a dictionary definition of discretion,' said Thane softly. 'But I've got my own. I call it mixing common sense with a hunch and maybe a flavour of humanity – when you can afford the humanity. But use it, and the responsibility for what happens afterwards is all yours.'

He'd finished. Sergeant Easter's hoarse bellow brought the class up from their desks, then, as he dismissed them, they began drifting out of the lecture room. The canteen was open and it was coffee-break time. Hanging back a little, the lanky probationer named Deacon hesitated and for a moment Thane thought he was going to come over. Then the redhead called to Deacon from the doorway and he gave a grin and followed her out.

'Nice as always, sir,' said Sergeant Easter as Thane stuffed his lecture notes into an inside pocket. Easter, plump and in his forties, spoke in a husky, almost strangled voice. He'd talked that way ever since a thug had kicked him in the throat one dark, back-street night when he'd been a beat cop. Afterwards, he'd been posted to the Training Centre staff – and a decade of intakes ever since had known him as the Easter Bunny. 'That bit about discretion was new, wasn't it?'

'I felt that way.' Thane's mouth tightened a little as he remembered the reason. Three days before a thin, middle-aged housewife had been brought into Millside Division on a petty shop-lifting charge. She'd been weeping, she'd had a child by the hand, and it had only taken a couple of telephone calls plus her promise to pay for the whole matter to be dropped.

It was only later he'd discovered she had five previous convictions over in Govan Division, where she was known as Weeping Winnie.

'Aye, well maybe some of it sinks in,' said Easter doubtfully, then grinned. 'Most of those lads are more interested in who'll manage to lay our redhead.'

Thane raised a quizzical eyebrow.

'Not a chance,' declared Easter hoarsely, and winked. 'She's as cool as an iceberg – but she's got them all jumping on a string and she knows it. That's a girl who'll go places.'

'We've never had a female Chief Constable,' murmured Thane, then glanced at his watch. 'Time I got out of here and back to Millside.'

Sergeant Easter escorted him from the lecture room and along a corridor past other doors where other groups in the Training Centre's constantly changing population were still busy. Some classrooms housed probationers nearing the end of their two-year term and ready to graduate as full constables. Behind other doors, experienced men of widely varied rank were on brief refresher courses on subjects as widely varied as Support Group tactics and drug-abuse prevention.

Down in the basement was the firearms range. Scottish police still didn't carry arms but more and more it was policy to have a considerable percentage of men trained to marksman standard in their use . . . and sometimes they were needed.

The far end of the corridor led out into the college yards. Mild April sunlight streamed down on a squad of men being drilled by another sergeant and they skirted them, heading for the row of cars parked on the far side. The drill sergeant winked at Thane as he passed, then drew a deep breath and snarled out new commands to the boot-slamming rookies.

The drill sergeant had fought against Thane years back when they were both young, new beat cops who liked boxing. The drill sergeant had twice made the Scottish police championship title and twice knocked out Thane in the process.

But most people who met Colin Thane, whatever the circumstances, remembered him. Professionally, he rated as the youngest and among the most successful Divisional C.I.D. chiefs in the city. Physically, he topped the six-foot mark and was burly to match.

Burly without being overweight, though he'd put on a few pounds since his days in the ring. Still in his early forties, he walked with an athletic ease which dated back to that earlier time.

He had dark hair which his two children were gradually persuading him to leave longer than his normal close-clipped cut. His face was tanned, could politely be classed as interestingly rugged, and he had brown, at times surprisingly thoughtful, eyes. The cream shirt and blue tie he wore had been a belated Christmas present his wife had bought him at the winter sales and went with a lightweight grey tweed suit and suede shoes.

The rest came down to a reputation for an unorthodox outlook which brought an uneasy reaction from Headquarters even when things went right. As for when they went wrong . . .

At least they weren't likely to hear about Weeping Winnie. She was on Thane's mind as he crossed to his car, a two-year-old Hillman station wagon which had rust round the doors and a spare tyre with only a memory of tread.

A sudden, uncharacteristic rumble of anger from Sergeant Easter brought him back to his surroundings.

'I'll have his guts, so help me,' croaked Easter, scowling past Thane's car. 'Damn him, he's been warned often enough.'

The object of his annoyance was further along the line, a small red Mini Cooper with a megaphone exhaust, knobbled rally tyres, two bold white roof stripes and a garland of extra spotlamps up front. Thane walked towards it, grinning. The Mini Cooper was scarred and battered but obviously in the 'tuned with loving care' category. Its long, flexible radio aerial had a tiny Snoopy pennant tied to the tip.

'Yours, Sergeant?' he asked mildly.

Easter wasn't amused.

'Robby Deacon's,' he said shortly. 'One o' the new intake. You'd maybe noticed him, sir. Tall, thin like he was hung together with wire, dark hair –'

'I noticed him,' nodded Thane, the grin lingering. 'He seemed a good each-way bet with the Manson girl.'

'He's a good each-way bet to feel my boot.' Easter frowned at the car as if he hoped it would vanish. 'He knows he should keep this damned whizz-bang somewhere else. Parking in the yard is for senior officers only and always has been.'

'Sacred ground,' agreed Thane cheerfully. 'We've few enough privileges. Somebody better sort out Constable Deacon before he gets any more delusions of grandeur.'

'Aye.' The Easter Bunny smiled grimly and had his own little moment of revenge. 'Sooner the better. We started him on uniformed beat training last week – in your division, Mr Thane.'

Thane grimaced, wondering which unfortunate Uniformed Branch section sergeant had been landed with the job. C.I.D. didn't see the rookies and Uniformed Branch usually tried to hide them somewhere quiet while they were still in the early probationer stage, mixing college sessions with beat work.

He considered the Mini Cooper with a more thoughtful interest. It was old, but it was business-like. The dashboard had extra instruments and a scatter of auxiliary switches and it had a leather-rimmed light alloy steering wheel. A home-made roll-over cage of steel tubing had been fitted under the roof line, the rear seat had been removed, and the space was occupied by two extra spare wheels, a shovel, petrol cans, and a jumble of tools and equipment.

'I've heard he's good at this motor-sport stuff,' admitted Easter wryly. 'But damn it, he's a cop now.'

'How would you rate him – as a cop?' asked Thane. 'Difficult.'

'Meaning?' Thane raised an eyebrow. The Easter Bunny had an uncanny ability when it came to making forecasts about his rookie material.

Easter shrugged. 'He's the best in that intake on ability. But turn your back on him and he'll invent half a dozen reasons for dodging work. One way or another, he'll be worth watching.'

'The Traffic mob can always use a good driver,' mused Thane.

'He wants to make C.I.D.,' said Easter stonily. Something in his hoarse voice made it plain that he felt C.I.D. was as good a dumping ground as any for problem cops.

'Thanks for the warning,' said Thane dryly. 'I like to know when someone's after my job.'

He said goodbye to Easter, returned to his own car, and a few moments later was driving out of the college.

It was an old, Victorian, stone-faced building, gutted to give a modern interior which included its own closed-circuit TV studio area. The streets around were a mixture of derelict slum tenements, cleared sites and brand-new high-rise apartment blocks.

Some unknown but practically minded Victorian planner had sited Glasgow's Police Training Centre in

11

the heart of the notorious Gorbals ghetto. Generations of rookies had found all the rough-and-tumble experience they needed waiting just beyond the front door.

But now, like a lot more of Glasgow's disastrous legacy of slumland, the old Gorbals had almost gone. Most of its neds – the city's tag for small-time hoodlums – had emigrated with their families to be rehoused elsewhere, taking their violence with them to the new areas. What was left of the Gorbals had been partly taken over by a gentler breed, Indian or Pakistani shopkeepers or bus-drivers. They worked hard, their womenfolk were shy and wore saris or bright silks, and so far they were still few enough in number to pose no integration problem.

There was even a garden area of trees and shrubs and grass at Gorbals Cross, the one-time gangland meeting place. A sign said 'Keep Off the Grass' – and it was generally respected, even when the neds came back to visit on Saturday nights and fights broke out.

The Gorbals hadn't been tamed. It was still part of the same old tinderbox, unpredictably violent city. But grass and trees were precious to people brought up among concrete and rats.

Twenty minutes later, after driving across town, Colin Thane arrived at Millside Division police office and left his car in the private parking lot. The pale spring sunshine sparkled on some broken glass near the entrance and the usual debris of torn paper and other rubbish stirred in the light wind, trapped against the compound wire.

Millside police office was in that kind of area and matched it, a grimy slab of mock-Gothic architecture built of grey granite which had spawned brick extensions over the years and sprouted a tall communications aerial from the roof. But in another few months it would be empty. The Division was having a new home built nearer the docks, where some old warehouses had been pulled down.

Thane reached the main door of the station building. One of the posters on the noticeboard had been removed since morning – an appeal for information about a double murder over in Eastern Division. It wasn't needed any more. The man they'd wanted had been fished out of the River Clyde with his pockets full of stones.

Two constables came out, saluted as they saw him, and he nodded a greeting then went into the building. Passing the Uniformed Branch inquiry counter and the clicking static of the radio room, he went quickly up the main stairway and into C.I.D. territory.

Millside C.I.D. operated from a big, open-plan room which had a couple of private offices at the far end. The furnishings were plain and scarred, the walls were painted cream every second year, and the heavy brown linoleum had had paths worn on it by generations of use.

As usual in late afternoon, things seemed quiet. Most of the day-shift squad were out on inquiries, a shirt-sleeved detective constable sat pecking out a report on a typewriter, another was on the telephone, and Detective Sergeant MacLeod, the shift sergeant, was at his desk talking quietly to a well-dressed woman who was clutching a handbag as if her life depended on maintaining that grip.

Thane's office door was lying open. He went in, and the slight, shabby figure standing pawing through the stacked papers on his desk half-turned. Detective Inspector Phil Moss, second-in-command, gave a grunt which was meant to be a welcome.

'What have we lost now?' asked Thane mildly, coming round and dropping into the battered swivel chair he'd inherited from his predecessor, whose wife had had connections in the furniture trade. 'Relax, Phil – you look like you're expecting Doomsday tomorrow.'

'If we were, you'd forget where you'd put the memo about it.' Moss abandoned his search and scowled. 'While you were telling the story of your life to an admiring audience I had the City Architect's Department round, wanting to talk about the new building. I couldn't even find the flaming plan!'

'It's around somewhere,' said Thane vaguely, wondering what the City Architect's delegation had made of Moss with his rumpled clothes and down-at-heel air. Moss frequently looked as though he'd slept in what he was wearing. Thane suspected he sometimes did. 'I remember putting it away, Phil.'

'That's a help,' said Moss sarcastically. He paused and gave a long, rumbling belch, loud enough to be heard beyond the partitioning out in the main office. 'Where's somewhere?'

Ignoring the belch, Thane tried to think and began opening drawers. Phil Moss's duodenal ulcer and the way he fought off any suggestion of surgical treatment with a wild variety of do-it-yourself remedies was legend in every police division in the city. But when it came to organization and detail Moss remained the methodical half of their team – despite his appearance.

The two men varied all along the line. Moss was older, somewhere vaguely in his late fifties but refusing to admit he even had a birthday. Small, thin, naturally pale, with thinning, mousy hair, there was a legend that he'd got past the minimum height standard at his entry medical by standing on tiptoe. A determined bachelor with a grey, acid view of life in general, his name brought a natural grin to people

14

who knew him. But the grins didn't mask their respect for his sheer, burrowing ability as a cop.

Phil Moss might look like a social security case. His complaining insolence, often fed by that grumbling ulcer, could be abrasive. Yet from the moment he and Thane had come together at Millside he'd worked without a hint of resentment at being outranked by a younger man. What had begun as a successful professional amalgam had developed into a wry brand of friendship.

'Found it.' Thane dragged the missing plan from deep down at the bottom of a drawer and tossed it on the desk. The folded paper had a dried tea-stain across it from a couple of nights back. 'All right, what else did I miss?'

'Not much.' Moss caught the cigarette Thane tossed him, accepted a light, and grimaced as he took a first draw of the smoke. 'We'd a minor panic about a knife-fight on a Spanish ship down at the docks, though it was broken up before it really mattered. They're both in the cells, but I've cut myself worse shaving. Another rent collector got mugged out at Fortrose –'

'Who's on that?' Thane frowned. Being a rent collector out there was becoming a hazardous occupation.

'D.C. Beech.' Moss grimaced his own dislike of the notion. 'He was about all I had available. Mac has a widow from Monkswalk on his plate. Her house was robbed while she was at a coffee-morning – jewellery and stuff, but she's insured.'

'Let's hope she enjoyed the coffee.' Thane remembered the well-dressed woman he'd seen with Sergeant MacLeod. At least she wasn't another shoplifter. 'Well, it'll give her something to talk about.'

He let his cigarette burn for a moment, glancing pensively at the crime map on the wall. Millside

15

Division lay like a great, oblong slab on the city's north-west, stretching from dockland out into the well-heeled suburbs. A parish of some hundred thousand people, from neds who'd steal anything that wasn't nailed down to expensively suited executives who produced their own brand of crime.

Millside was a sandwich of industrial areas and slums, low-rental city housing developments like Fortrose and high amenity colonies like Monkswalk. But it all came down to people, and a bank balance wasn't supposed to be any part of a cop's guide to respectability.

'One thing didn't happen,' said Moss suddenly, cutting across his thoughts. 'That girl didn't call back – the one who tried to get you yesterday.'

'Doreen Ashton?' Thane had the name circled on his desk pad. Who she was, he didn't know. But she'd telephoned Millside twice the previous afternoon, asking for him by name. He'd been out at the time, Moss hadn't been around, and the duty orderly had only managed to coax from her that she wanted to talk about something important and confidential, plus a promise that she'd phone again that afternoon. 'Then there's not much we can do about it.'

'If it matters, we'll hear soon enough.' Moss stabbed a thin finger towards the plan on the desk. 'The City Architect's people will be back again tomorrow. They've hit a snag.'

'Another one?' Thane raised a cynical eyebrow. Anything connected with the new building seemed a problem. 'What's wrong this time?'

'Something about the elevator shaft. They've got to move it – which probably means dropping the thing through where your room was going to be.' Moss scratched himself gloomily under one armpit. 'I told them that had possibilities, but they weren't amused.'

16

Thane grinned then looked round as they heard a knock on the door. It opened, and the duty orderly brought in the afternoon despatches from Headquarters. Once the man had gone, he opened them.

There wasn't much that mattered to Millside. He tossed the latest stolen property list across to Moss, who would get some luckless plain-clothes man to make the usual trudge round the pawn shops. A circular from Chief Superintendent Ilford, head of the city's C.I.D. force, amounted to a warning about excessive overtime claims, and some superintendent he'd never heard of at Headquarters wanted Divisional statistics on the recovery of stolen cars.

He consigned Ilford's note to the waste bucket and marked the statistics query for the attention of Uniformed Branch, knowing they'd try to heave it straight back at him.

'Phil, have you heard anything about a rookie named Robby Deacon?' he asked for no particular reason.

'No.' Moss had drifted over to the window and answered without looking round. 'Why?'

'Seems he's here doing beat training with the uniformed side. I came across him at that lecture session.' Thane stubbed his cigarette and glanced at his watch, his mind already moving on. 'The Easter Bunny says he wants to make C.I.D.'

'If he does, he's a mental case.' Moss turned in time to see Thane shoving back his chair and rising. 'Going out?'

'Going home,' corrected Thane with a wisp of a grin. 'Mary and the kids are going to a swimming gala tonight – something to do with school. I thought I'd go along too.'

'Break the news gently,' said Moss dryly. 'The shock might be bad for them.' Rubbing his chin, he nodded.

17

'I'll be around for a spell if that girl should call. Eh . . . anything else likely to happen?'

'No, and try and keep it that way,' pleaded Thane, heading for the door. 'I promised I'd make this swimming thing.'

'Then don't fall in the pool,' advised Moss woodenly. 'You're too damned big to pull out again unless they've a crane handy.'

'Stuff your crane,' said Thane cheerfully, and went out.

Once the door closed, Moss turned back to his view from the window. Across the street, children were playing on vacant ground where a row of tenements had been pulled down. When that happened, some of the rats that escaped had tried to set up home in the Millside office and the divisional cat had worked overtime. But there were plenty of other long rows of tenements beyond the vacant ground, their backyards exposed, washing hung out to dry here and there in the sunlight.

His stomach had a nagging ache again, a direct legacy of having to settle for a rushed pie-and-beans lunch at a snack bar down the road.

At least they were promised a built-in restaurant with waitress service when they moved to the new Millside office, whenever that might be. But Phil Moss had his doubts on some other aspects.

The new office would have computer links to Headquarters, facsimile print-out facilities, decent interview rooms, better technical facilities. The City Architect's team had even talked proudly about a shower block attached to the cells for prisoners' use.

With luck, he supposed, the occasional cop might be allowed to use it too.

His narrow, grey eyes strayed down to the Divisional office's main door. The stone arch was topped by a typically Victorian statue of a heavily robed female. She was supposed to represent the spirit of justice and it wasn't her fault that the way the robes bulged around her middle section resulted in her being known as Expectant Ethel.

He'd miss Ethel. But you couldn't reckon on any of the long-haired wonders from the City Architect's Department understanding about her when they were having hysterics about things like misplaced elevator shafts.

Moss's stomach kicked a new warning. Feeling in a jacket pocket, he brought out a small, dark-green pill shaped like a torpedo.

He was taking half a dozen a day and the course was supposed to last a month. They came from a new Organic Foods store that had opened near the boarding house he called home.

It could have been a lot more homely if he'd wanted. His landlady had been scheming round that possibility for years, from darning his underwear to trying to get him to buy even one new suit.

Moss swallowed the pill with a grimace. A compound of extract of rhubarb, something called bee's elixir and charcoal, it tasted vile enough to have to do some good.

The taste was still with him as Thane's telephone rang. He went over to the desk, answered it, and found Detective Constable Beech was on the line from Fortrose housing scheme.

'This rent collector who was supposed to be mugged, sir,' began Beech happily. 'He's a fake. I've been tailing him and he's just collected the rent bag from behind a dustbin. Will I bring him in?'

Moss drew a deep breath. Beech was young, enthusiastic, the father of months-old twins, and incapable of producing the expected.

'Bring him in – why?' he snarled down the line. 'Give him his bus fare home, like we usually do.'

Suddenly, he had a startled notion of Beech doing just that. 'No, collect him, you idiot. And bring the damned bag while you're at it.'

He felt better as he hung up. Maybe it was the pill, maybe not. He'd forgotten to ask what had made Beech follow the man in the first place, but that could wait.

Going back to the window, Moss noticed the way the sun had begun colouring the grey slates of the distant tenement roof-tops. They looked as warm and clean and red as traffic lights.

It made, he decided, a pleasant end to a peaceful day.

Mary Thane had picked her outfit with care for the swimming gala, though any of the other school mothers around with long memories had seen most of her wardrobe several times over. She wore a light, short-length camel coat with a tie belt over a dark blue pinafore dress which had a red silk scarf cravat style at the throat, her shoes at least were near enough to new, and her big bucket bag was dictated by the inevitable family outing emergency needs.

She had long, dark hair and a smooth, fresh complexion. Her neat figure made a nonsense of the years she'd been married and the fact she had two school-age children. Any time Colin Thane thought about it, he guessed that she even took the same size in dresses . . . and that she'd probably claim they were the same dresses and had to be on a cop's pay.

At the swimming gala they had seats halfway up the main spectator gallery. The gala was shaping to be a success, meaning the right team was winning, and Thane found they were both being caught up in the excitement, parental inhibitions forgotten, as the tussle between the two schools reached its climax.

Young Tommy Thane managed a respectable second place in the fifty metres butterfly final while his sister Kate pranced and shouted round the edge of the pool waving a large Teddy bear mascot in their school colours. Then they vanished, except to reappear from time to time to borrow money for more hot dogs.

At last, the prizes presented and the gala over, the Thane family somehow reunited in the general exodus and, complete with the mascot bear, drove home through the darkened streets.

Most of the time was occupied by the excited chatter coming from the rear seat. It was still going on as Thane swung the car into their driveway. Home was a small bungalow in a street where everything was identical about the houses except the colour of the do-it-yourself paint jobs and the layout of the handkerchief-sized gardens. Plus, the more cynical would have added, the amount of the mortgages.

Thane carried the bear mascot into the house as his share of the loads, then turned up the heating and switched on the TV. He heard Mary fighting a patient battle which ended with the two youngsters admitting defeat and going to bed, then she came through and flopped down on the couch beside him, laughing.

'What's so funny?' he demanded.

'Our two.' Mary shook her head. 'Tommy told Kate he'll go for gold at the next Olympics, then turn professional. Now they're rowing about how much commission she'd get as his manager.' She looked around, slightly surprised. 'Where's the dog?'

'In his basket in the porch.'

'Good.' The dog was a large unruly Boxer, called Clyde as a reminder of the rivulets of wet it had made as a pup. Mary settled back, drawing up her knees and clasping her hands round them, relaxing, still smiling.

21

'I'm glad you managed tonight, Colin,' she said suddenly. 'You said you would, but –' She didn't need to finish.

He grinned. 'They're my kids too, remember. Like a drink to celebrate?'

'It's late.' She pouted her lips for a moment, considering. 'All right. We'll celebrate a famous victory. Then I'll get some supper.'

He poured the drinks and brought them back to the couch.

'Supper wasn't what I had in mind,' he said mildly.

'No?' She looked up at him, a different kind of teasing laughter in her eyes.

And the telephone began ringing.

Her expression crumpled at the sound. Shrugging at the inevitable, Thane turned and went out into the hall. He lifted the receiver and the voice at the other end was the night switchboard operator at Millside Division, apologetic as always.

'Inspector Moss told me to contact you, sir. He's at Leyland Street with what looks like a murder – and he says sorry, but he'd like you to join him there.'

'When did it happen?' asked Thane wearily.

'First report was about an hour ago, sir.' The operator's voice made it clear that she, at least, knew there was a difference. 'We tried to contact you earlier.'

'I was out.' Thane knew Leyland Street. It ran through an area of rented apartments and quiet terrace houses, seldom featuring on the crime map. 'Get a car to collect me and pass a message to Inspector Moss that I'm on my way.'

He hung up, not bothering to ask who else had been alerted. If Phil Moss was there, it would already have been done.

When he turned from the telephone he found Mary standing a few feet away, where she'd been listening. Like him, she was still holding her drink in one hand.

22

'Cheers,' he said wryly, lifting his glass.

One thing was certain. He wouldn't even see supper now.

It was a few minutes after midnight when the Millside duty car reached Leyland Street and pulled in to join half a dozen other vehicles already parked under the street lamps beside a patch of waste ground. Thane climbed out at the kerb, told his driver to stay on radio watch, and glanced around to establish his bearings.

The open ground seemed about a hundred yards wide and was flanked on either side by the blank gable walls of terrace houses. There were lights and people at some of the house windows. For some, at least, the night appeared likely to offer some unexpected free entertainment.

Further in, the waste ground broadened and stretched away to where there were other street lamps and houses. Some kind of path appeared to run across it and he noted for later that the backs of the distant houses probably had the best view of the area.

But what mattered first was a derelict car which lay maybe seventy yards in from where he was standing. A Scientific Bureau battery spotlamp was already shining on its remains, showing the flattened, useless tyres, doors which sagged open on their hinges, and broken glass frosting the ground around.

The men around the car were concentrating on the luggage boot, which had its lid raised. He saw them ease back and the quick spit of light as a camera's electronic flash seared the darkness.

Thane started walking towards them. A uniformed constable stepped out of the shadows to challenge him then just as quickly faded back again, saluting. Other details registered as he got nearer. Doc

Williams, the police surgeon, was there. The bulky figure beside the Scientific Bureau cameraman was Dan Laurence, the superintendent in charge of the Bureau . . . and Dan Laurence usually only turned out when things appeared likely to be unusually interesting.

He'd been seen. He heard a shout, then saw Phil Moss coming to meet him. At the same time, Thane slowed and sniffed the air as the acrid odours of hot oil and burnt paint reached his nostrils. Something else was there too, something even more unpleasant, and his stomach tightened as he recognized it.

'Aye, Colin.' Moss's nod of greeting was minimal and his thin face was hard to read in the night. But his voice was unemotionally grey. 'Takeover time, 00.10 hours, okay?'

Thane glanced at his wrist watch and nodded agreement. There had been an Edinburgh murder trial the previous month when defence counsel had made a big play about timings. Tightening up had been a natural reflex all round.

'What have we got, Phil?' he asked.

'Problems.' Moss stuck his hands deep in the pockets of his old raincoat. 'Do you want to look first or hear about it?'

'Your version, no padding.' Thane lit a cigarette in sheer reflex action, heard Moss's blatantly protesting throat-clearance, and brought out the pack again. 'Like one?'

'Thanks.' Moss also needed a light. He took a first draw, the cigarette's red tip glowing, and let the smoke out slowly. 'There's a dead girl in the car's luggage boot, Colin. Age early twenties, nothing to identify her – Doc Williams reckons she's been dead at least twenty-four hours.'

'How was she found?'

'A long-shot chance, with the local beat cop on the sharp end of it, poor sod.' Moss almost grinned. 'He was near here, heard a hell of a bang and came running – a couple of youngsters had been dropping lighted matches down the car's fuel-filler pipe to see what would happen, and there was just enough vapour left in the tank to turn it into a king-sized firecracker.'

'So?' Thane kept his patience, knowing he was getting the story tightly compressed, that Moss had a reason for every word.

'The kids had minor burns and shock, so the beat man used his personal radio to call an ambulance. He didn't bother about the fire brigade, because the car didn't do much more than smoulder for a few minutes. Then, once the kids had been ferried off to hospital, he took a last prowl around the car.

'The boot lid seemed to have sprung open with the blast, he happened to shine his torch at it, saw what was inside – and pressed the panic button.'

Thane could imagine. Moss at his side, he walked the rest of the distance towards the car. It was a Volvo saloon, or what was left of one. Abandoned cars were quickly pillaged for spares.

'Hello, Colin. I was wondering when you'd show up.' The untidy bear of a man who stepped forward to greet him wore a vast sheepskin jacket and seemed cheerful. Dan Laurence always preferred a job which gave the Scientific Bureau something out of the ordinary. 'What kept you, man?'

'A night off. My family have odd notions about liking to see me now and again,' said Thane dryly.

'Mine too.' Laurence frowned around. 'Well, we've done what we can for now. But I'd like this whole damned chunk of waste ground closed to the peasant hordes if you can manage it. Doc Williams has a notion about what happened, and –'

'What do you mean, a notion?' demanded the police surgeon's indignant voice. Doc Williams came over from the Volvo, wiping his hands on a cloth which smelled strongly of antiseptic. He wore a black tie and dinner jacket and grimaced as he saw Thane's eyebrows rise. 'I got hauled out of a Rotary Club dance for this. I'd call that bad enough without having the tradesmen trying to be critical.'

Thane considered the two men with a wisp of a grin, knowing their delight at scoring points, knowing it was part of their defence against the realities they dealt in.

'So let's have the professional verdict, Doc,' he invited.

'First, she's been dead about twenty-four hours. That's calculated on body temperature and the degree of rigor – though of course I want to make that only a provisional conclusion.'

'Naturally,' murmured Laurence cynically. 'Hedge your bets, boy.'

Doc Williams sniffed and tried to ignore him. 'Second, the blast may have jarred the boot lid open, but the metal shielded her from the flash and whatever amount of burning occurred afterwards – at worst, she's only slightly crisped at the edges. Not enough to complicate an autopsy.' He paused and beckoned Thane. 'I'll show you the rest of what I mean.'

Moss had drifted over to talk to a couple of C.I.D. men near the front of the car. Thane left him there and followed the police surgeon over to the luggage boot. The full glare of the battery spotlight shone down on it and he looked, his mouth tightening.

The dead girl had been bundled head-first into the compartment and lay doubled up on her side with her knees almost against her chin. Her hair was long and dark and obscured most of her face. She was slim, certainly young, and the way her blue mini dress had rumpled high, almost to her waist, made an additional obscenity to her death. The rest of her clothing was a white, mildly scorched anorak jacket, badly ripped tights and a torn pair of floral cotton briefs.

'Here's what I mean,' said Doc Williams in a clinically conversational tone. 'Torn clothing, Colin, including the dress. Surface injuries to her throat and head – and some fairly deep scratch marks around the thighs. There's a clear enough possibility – an attempted rape that came unstuck.'

'Someone tried too hard,' grunted Dan Laurence behind them, the humour gone from his voice. 'I wouldn't quarrel with that, Colin. We can't find her shoes – or her handbag if she had one. They're among the reasons why I want this place sealed off till daylight.'

Turning away, Thane looked around. It was a reasonable enough theory and other possibilities stemmed from it. The girl could have been using the path across the waste ground as a shortcut, perhaps going home. Or she could have been there with a man for other reasons – reasons that got out of hand. He considered the nearest houses grimly. For all he knew, her killer might be among the people grandstanding from those lighted windows.

But somebody had killed her, then had hidden her body. Perhaps to move it again later, perhaps in sheer panic not caring how or when it would be found. Phil Moss was right. Whatever the truth, they had problems.

'Dan's team are finished here, Colin,' said Doc Williams. 'I'd like her moved to the mortuary whenever you're ready.' He glanced down at his dinner jacket and flicked a finger against his bow tie. 'No sense in going back to the party – I'll get out of this monkey suit and start working on her.'

'Arrange it, Doc,' agreed Thane quietly. 'Just give me a few minutes.'

He left them, went over to Moss, told him to organize cordoning off the entire area of waste ground, then asked, 'Where's the cop who found her, Phil?'

'Over there,' said Moss almost mildly, thumbing to their left. 'I – uh – think you know him.'

Puzzled, Thane started towards the uniformed figure standing just beyond the glare of light then stifled a grunt, understanding. It was Robby Deacon – and the lanky, dark-haired young rookie he'd last seen at the Training Centre looked white-faced and shaken.

'Sir.' Moistening his lips, Deacon stiffened.

'Relax, laddy,' said Thane briskly, keeping the sympathy from his voice. 'You've been dropped in at the deep end, I know. But at least it'll give you the edge on the Easter Bunny next time you're at college.'

'Yes, sir.' Deacon tried to grin but didn't quite make it.

Thane felt a momentary surge of fury at the situation. In theory, a probationer cop starting beat training should have been teamed to patrol with an experienced man. But it couldn't always work that way, Millside Division's Uniformed Branch was as undermanned as any – and he could imagine some harassed section sergeant deciding that the Leyland Street beat was quiet enough to risk turning over to a rookie on his own.

'I've heard what happened,' he said almost harshly, the thought still angering him. 'You seem to have kept your head all right. But now we're going to check a couple of details. Understood?'

Deacon nodded uncertainly.

'Tell me about the boot lid.'

'Yes, sir.' Deacon shuffled his feet, vaguely uneasy. 'That kind has a push-button lock. I reckon it was blown loose by the blast.'

'How wide was it open?'

Deacon swallowed. 'An inch or two, maybe. But –'

'But you didn't just bend down and do a keyhole act with your torch, did you?' Thane eyed him woodenly. 'What made you open it wider?'

'Well –' Deacon moistened his lips again – 'I suppose I was just curious, sir. I'm keen on cars.'

'Keen enough to wonder if there was anything inside worth scrounging?' asked Thane softly.

'Not particularly, sir. I – well, I just did it.'

'Come on.' Thane beckoned and led him back to the car. 'Did you touch the girl at all? Think hard.'

'No, sir.' Deacon shook his head emphatically.

'All right. Then show me how the lid was lying.'

His eyes avoiding the dead girl, Deacon reached for the lid and started to bring it down. It stuck and after a moment's hesitation he bent and glanced in at the hinges. Gripping a support, he twisted it, then started to rise again.

Then he froze, staring at the dead girl, his mouth hanging open. With a strange air of compulsion and horrified reluctance he reached out a hand and gently brushed aside some of the long, dark hair which still hid most of her face.

He stepped back slowly, still staring at the girl, then turned blindly and blundered off – away from the car, out into the darkness. Staring after him, Thane heard an all too-familiar retching noise.

The other men working around said nothing, but exchanged glances. Phil Moss strolled over to join Thane and shrugged.

'He'll learn,' was Moss's comment.

Thane nodded and they waited till Deacon came back. The lanky rookie still had flecks of vomit on his tunic.

'I'm sorry, sir,' he said in an almost ashamed voice.

'Don't be,' Thane told him.

'I know her, sir,' said Deacon simply.

29

An odd gurgling noise came from Moss. Thane swallowed, but, prompted by their expressions, Deacon spoke again.

'I mean it, sir. I – I hadn't looked at her really close up before. What I saw the first time was enough.'

'You're sure?' Moss half-glanced towards the car. 'Maybe you'd better have another look and –'

'No, sir.' Deacon shook his head. 'I know her all right. Her name is Doreen Ashton – she lives near here.'

'Doreen Ashton –' Thane glanced at Moss.

'Bloody hell,' said Moss softly.

They were both thinking of the telephone call that hadn't materialized that afternoon. Of the girl named Doreen Ashton who had tried to contact Thane not much more than twenty-four hours before but who had failed.

'What do you know about her?' asked Thane greyly.

'She's a girl who hangs around the same car club as I do, sir,' said Deacon, too busy with his own thoughts to notice their reaction. 'She – well, she hasn't a car but she helps.' He looked over at the boot, then quickly switched back to them. 'I – in fact I was even talking to her last night. Just – well, just chatting.'

'Where?' demanded Moss, frowning.

'Out of town, near Drymen.' Deacon grimaced weakly, trying to explain. 'A bunch of us from the car club were helping to set up markers and other gear on one of the forest roads – it's going to be used in a rally route at the weekend.'

'Weren't you on duty last night?' asked Thane.

'No, sir.' Deacon hesitated. 'She was still there when I left. I – well, left early.' He saw Thane's raised eyebrow. 'I had some work to do on my car, in fact I was at it till about one a.m.'

'Where?' asked Moss again.

'In a lock-up garage I rent.' Deacon grimaced. 'Repairs are do-it-yourself on a cop's pay.'

Thane nodded agreement. 'Back to the girl. 'You're sure she lives near here?'

Deacon frowned uncertainly across the waste ground to the street lights on the far side. 'I know she shared a flat with a couple of other girls over there – I think it's in Swanhill Street.'

'Who took her out to this rally route?' asked Thane slowly.

'I'm not sure, sir.' Deacon shook his head. 'Probably it would be her boss, Duncan MacRath. Maybe you've heard of him.'

'No,' said Moss flatly. 'Tell us.'

'Well –' Deacon managed a weak smile. 'He's got something to do with the whisky trade, but mainly he's a top-line rally driver.'

Moss grunted, unimpressed. 'Where do we find him?'

'Duncan?' Deacon appeared bewildered. 'His family have a big place out near Helensburgh – Glenrath House. But –'

'But what?' demanded Thane.

'Well, he's all right, sir,' said Deacon awkwardly.

'Did I say he wasn't?' Thane eyed him bleakly. 'Tell your section sergeant I'm sending you back to Millside for the rest of your shift. You'll write a full report – anything you've ever known or heard about this girl, everything that happened while you were at Drymen last night. That's all, Constable.'

'Sir.' Deacon stiffened again, snapped a salute which was textbook style in its indignation, and went off looking hurt.

'Well?' asked Moss after a moment. 'Do we sniff around this Duncan MacRath character, or are we looking for a stray nut-case?'

'Right now, we keep all the options open, Phil.' Colin Thane was looking down towards Leyland Street, where Deacon was now talking to a uniformed sergeant. All the options – Robby Deacon included. At this stage, they had to play it that way.

Moss grunted. 'Want me to collect MacRath?'

'Why rush it?' asked Thane wryly. 'But I don't mind spoiling his night's sleep. Get the local cops to dig him out of bed and tell him about the girl – and that we'll want him in the morning.' He paused and changed his mind. 'No, we'll tread easy. Make it we'll come to see him.'

'Why the friendly neighbourhood cop routine?' asked Moss suspiciously. 'Anything I don't know about?'

'Nothing,' said Thane truthfully. 'But that girl tried to contact me, Phil.' He shrugged. 'That's maybe where we should start – with the girl.'

Moss thought about it and nodded. Then he gave a belch and wandered off towards the cars.

Chapter Two

Robby Deacon had said the girl stayed somewhere in Swanhill Street and Thane took that job. Beckoning a spare detective constable to come along, he set off through the darkness towards the far side of the waste ground. They emerged under the yellow sodium glare of the street lights there and found Swanhill Street about another minute's walk along.

It was a long row of three-storey terrace houses, most of them converted into middle-income apartments. Locating the one Doreen Ashton had called home involved ringing doorbells at the first couple of houses where they saw lights. A party was in progress at the first, and they drew a blank. At the second, the bell was answered by a skinny young man wearing a beard and underpants who looked at Thane's warrant card with a wary suspicion, listened, then nodded.

'Dark hair, good looks and smart with it – yes, I know her,' he agreed.

'Know who, Pete?' A girl's tousled head showed round a door further down the hallway, followed by shoulders that had been hastily wrapped in a bed-sheet. 'Who is it?'

'Police,' said Pete hastily. 'They're looking for some-one.'

The head disappeared with a yelp.

'My – uh – sister,' said the young man awkwardly. 'You know how it goes – she's shy of strangers. But if you want Doreen Ashton you go to the next corner. She shares the basement flat there with a couple of girls – another couple of good-lookers.' His curiosity grew. 'What's up?'

'Nothing for you or your – uh – sister to worry about,' said Thane dryly.

'The "just routine" bit?' The beard was tugged knowingly. 'Surprise, surprise. She doesn't look the type to have the fuzz calling round.'

The detective constable at Thane's side stirred with a growl. His name was Lamont, he didn't talk much, but he had a daughter about Doreen Ashton's age.

'How old is that girl you've got in there, son?' he asked curtly. 'Do you know the law about minors?'

The grinning mouth fell slack with alarm.

'Tell her we'll maybe check on the way back,' agreed Thane woodenly. 'And thanks.'

They turned and walked away, hearing the door slam hastily behind them.

It was easy enough to find the basement flat. It had its own little stairway down from street level, there were lights behind the closed curtains and they could hear a radio playing. They went down to the door, which was painted a bold blue and white, and Thane used the ornamental brass knocker.

The radio was switched off, a curtain twitched briefly, then after a moment the door opened a few inches on a security chain. The girl who looked out was fair-haired and wore a quilted dressing gown.

'Police,' said Thane, and showed his warrant card again.

'We don't need any,' the girl said firmly. 'What do you want?'

'It's about Doreen Ashton,' said Thane patiently.

'Doreen?' They heard a quick intake of breath, then the security chain rattled loose and the door opened wide. Her face glistening with some kind of overnight

34

cream, the girl in the dressing gown stared at them anxiously. 'Has something happened to her?'

Thane nodded slightly. 'Can we come in?'

'Yes, I – yes, of course.' She let them in, closed the door again, then gestured them on. 'Through here.'

They followed her into a small sitting room. It was brightly furnished in pop-art style with posters on the walls and folk-weave rugs on the floors.

'I'm Jenny Fallon.' The girl, plump but pretty, with a snub nose, moistened her lips. 'If Doreen's in any kind of trouble –'

'Did she sleep here last night?' asked Thane quietly.

'No. But –'

'Have you a photograph of her, Miss Fallon?'

The girl's eyes widened. She went over to a sideboard and came back with a framed photograph, her hand trembling a little as she showed them it.

'That's Doreen on the left,' she said in a strained voice. 'The other girl is Mandy Ryan – she lives here too.'

The photograph showed three girls in swimsuits at a holiday beach, with Jenny Fallon in the middle. The girl on her right was a stranger with short dark hair and the other was the same girl they'd seen lying bundled and dead in the Volvo.

'Thanks,' said Thane quietly. 'Jenny, I'm sorry. I've got some bad news for you.'

'Bad?' Her face went white beneath the layer of complexion cream. 'You mean – you mean she's hurt?'

'She's dead, Jenny.'

For a moment she stared at them in sheer disbelief. Then, without a word, she turned slowly and replaced the photograph on the sideboard. She looked at it for another moment and blundered out of the room. Detective Constable Lamont took a half-step to follow her, but stopped where he was as Thane shook his head.

35

A couple of minutes passed while Lamont tried to appear interested in the pop-art posters and Thane lit a cigarette. At last the girl returned, still wearing the dressing gown but with red eyes. She had a handkerchief crumpled in one hand.

'You're quite sure?' she asked slowly. 'I mean, there couldn't be a mistake?'

'There's no mistake,' said Thane gently.

Jenny Fallon bit her lip, then sank into a gaily patterned beanbag chair and sat staring at the glowing bars of an electric fire.

'I didn't give you much of a welcome when you arrived,' she said wearily. 'I'm sorry – we've had some late-night problems lately and when I hear a knock at the door at this hour I get uptight.'

'What kind of problems?' asked Thane automatically.

'He's more a nuisance than a problem, I suppose,' she shrugged. 'We've a Peeping Tom prowling around. But he doesn't matter.' Turning to face them again, she asked, 'How did it happen – was it a road accident?'

'No.'

'Then –' She stopped, her bewilderment plain. 'I just thought –'

'She was murdered, Jenny.' Thane saw the new quiver of shock that went through the plump girl and wished he'd had a policewoman along, even just to hold Jenny Fallon's hand. 'We think she was killed last night. Her body was found about an hour ago.'

'Murdered.' Her mouth formed a tight, desperate line as she struggled for control and the hand holding the handkerchief tightened its grip until the knuckles showed white. 'But – but why?'

'As far as we can make out, she was attacked on the waste ground beside Leyland Street.' Thane exchanged a glance with Lamont and deliberately cut down on detail. 'Probably she was taking a shortcut back here. We don't know much more, except that her body was found in the luggage boot of an old car.'

'At Leyland Street – that old Volvo?' A new horror showed in her eyes as Lamont nodded. 'We always use that shortcut. I used it twice today. And she was –' Her voice faded, her own thoughts taking over.

'Now I need some help, Jenny.' Thane spoke almost harshly, forcing her to stay with him. 'Tell me about this prowler.'

'Just a kink of some kind,' she said with a bitter, helpless impatience. 'We've had him peeping at the windows or knocking at the door. Not often – just a few times. Three girls on their own are a natural for –' She stopped, suddenly understanding. 'Him?'

'It's too early to even start guessing.' Thane looked around, found an ashtray, and stubbed out his cigarette. 'What does this character look like, Jenny?'

She shook her head. 'We've just seen someone running away and it's always been late at night. I – well, I could meet him in the street and not know it.'

'That's likely enough,' said Lamont grimly. He was reaching for his notebook, but stopped as he saw Thane frown.

'When did this start?' asked Thane.

'About a couple of months ago. He usually appears at weekends.' By sheer physical effort she kept her voice steady. 'At first we thought it more of a joke than anything, having our own personal Peeping Tom. Doreen said – she said it would probably scare the hell out of him if we simply opened the door and invited him in.'

Thane frowned. 'Did you report this to anyone?'

'No.' She said it like a sigh. 'We talked about it, but all three of us felt we should stay quiet and hope he'd go away. You see, we've the kind of landlord who wouldn't appreciate any kind of fuss. We didn't want to risk being thrown out.'

Thane heard Lamont swear under his breath and felt the same way. He'd come across the same story often enough before – make a fuss and it might cause trouble. Trouble might mean the police becoming involved, which was something to be avoided at all costs.

'What about Mandy Ryan?' he asked at last, nodding towards the photograph. 'Where is she right now?'

'Mandy?' Jenny Fallon seemed to draw some comfort from the reminder. 'She's over in Ireland on holiday with her family for a few days. But she'll come straight back when she hears. We – well, the three of us have been very close, Chief Inspector.'

'Then how did you feel last night when Doreen didn't come home?' asked Thane bluntly. 'Weren't you worried then?'

'No.' She made a vague gesture with her hands. 'I knew she'd gone to help organize some car rally. She often did that.'

'Often helped or often didn't come home?' asked Lamont from the background.

'I didn't think you'd understand,' she said wearily. 'Sharing a flat, you have rules. One we had was that we were free to lead our own lives, no questions asked. I don't mean any of us went tarting around, but –'

'You didn't ask questions,' agreed Thane. 'Did Doreen have a steady boy friend?'

'Yes. He's at sea, an engineer on an oil tanker.' She bit her lip again. 'God knows where his ship is right now, but he'll need to be told too. They were talking about maybe getting engaged on his next leave.'

'We'll help with things like that,' promised Thane. There was one thing he still had to ask, something

38

he'd deliberately left till the finish. 'Think back over the last few days, Jenny. Did Doreen ever seem worried or upset, or did she talk about anything that was troubling her?'

'No, I don't remember anything.' The girl shook her head slowly. 'She was maybe quieter than usual, I suppose. But Doreen could be that way at times. She wasn't upset about our Peeping Tom, if that's what you mean – in fact, she laughed about him.'

Thane nodded slowly. 'Jenny, we can't find her shoes or a handbag. Could you check her things and see what's missing?'

The girl left them again for a couple of minutes, then returned.

'Doreen only had two handbags – they're both here. She often didn't carry one. I know her shoes, and the only pair missing are blue leather casuals with big metal buckles.'

'Thanks – and we'll leave it at that for now.' Thane touched her gently on the shoulder. 'I'll send a policewoman round, Jenny. She can keep you company till morning.'

As he spoke, the plump, complexion-creamed face seemed to crumple and the tears began running. Nodding to Lamont to follow him, Thane went out of the room and left the little basement apartment, making sure the blue and white outer door closed firmly behind them.

'Stay around and keep an eye on the place till that policewoman gets here,' he told Lamont once they were back on the street.

'Just in case, sir?' Lamont scowled his understanding. 'Sounds like we want this Peeping Tom, doesn't it?'

Thane shrugged. In his mind was a picture of three young, good-looking girls who had created their own private easy-going little world behind that blue and white door. It was a world that had just fallen apart at the seams.

He lit a fresh cigarette and walked away, glad that part was over.

A light, fine drizzle of rain began falling as Colin Thane reached the waste ground again and plunged back into its humped darkness, leaving the yellow glow of the streetlights behind him.

He was about a third of the way along the rough footpath, heading back towards the abandoned Volvo, when he had the sudden, uneasy feeling that he wasn't alone. He slowed, and this time heard it for certain – a rustle of movement which had nothing to do with the light wind or the rain. The sound came from over to his left, where the grass and weeds were high and thick, and it stopped as he stopped.

Deliberately, he dropped the stub of his cigarette and casually ground it underfoot. Then, still moving unhurriedly, he began walking towards the spot.

He was almost there when a dark-clad figure seemed to explode up out of the weeds, to crash off at a run in the opposite direction. Pounding after him, Thane shouted for the man to halt – but the only effect was to make his quarry increase his pace, rapidly widening the gap between them, covering the uneven, debris-littered ground like a greyhound fresh out of a trap.

Shouting again, Thane increased his effort. Then, suddenly, something firm yet pliant caught his right ankle, wrapped round it, and brought him crashing down on the ground. Swearing, he scrambled up, spent seconds freeing himself from a tangle of old wire, then looked around.

The man had gone. There was only the night, the ugly lumping contours of the waste ground, and the wavering beams of two torches heading towards him. The torches belonged to two uniformed constables who arrived panting a moment later. They stopped beside him, uncertain about what to do.

'You all right, sir?' asked one.

'Just fine,' grated Thane. 'But who the hell is supposed to be keeping people from wandering around this corner of the universe?'

The men exchanged a quick glance.

'We thought we saw something a few minutes back, sir,' said the same constable uneasily. 'But – well, we thought it was maybe a dog or something.'

His companion nodded quickly. 'Plenty of dogs wandering around here at night, sir.'

'Well, when I flushed this particular dog he moved on two feet and he ran like hell,' snarled Thane. 'He's medium height, medium build, wearing what looked like a black sweater and slacks. Start looking – and keep looking.'

They shuffled their feet, made noises that were meant to sound enthusiastic but fell short, and headed off. Thane sighed. He knew as well as they did that the prowler was well away. By now, he could be back in the safety of any one of the houses around. Or in any of the rows that lay beyond.

Murder always brought strange, unhappy beings out into the open. Some exposed twisted, secret fears and there were others for whom even a residual atmosphere of violence held a compulsive attraction.

But the man he'd just lost might equally easily have been the Peeping Tom whom Jenny Fallon had talked about. Somehow that Tom would have to be found.

Most times a Tom was a harmless oddity despite the way he alarmed and frightened. But there was always the outside chance, the kind that couldn't be ignored.

And Colin Thane couldn't forget that he'd let the running man get away.

At the Millside Division office the inevitable was waiting when he arrived. Headquarters had twice teleprinted impatient demands for a preliminary report on the Leyland Street murder. Uniformed Branch were making plaintive noises about the number of extra men needed if the waste ground around the car was to be sealed off for even a day.

On the way in, Thane had to get past the equally inevitable group of reporters being kept herded together at the ground-floor inquiry desk. He nodded at their plaintive reminders they had morning edition deadlines to meet and went up to C.I.D. territory.

There, just to help things along, he discovered that arson was suspected in a supermarket fire at the far end of King Street and an emergency call had come in from the docks about a second knife-fight aboard the Spanish ship.

He coped with the knife-fight first – foreign seamen meant consular officials, spluttering captains and occasional Interpol-type complications. The Millside C.I.D. cupboard was practically bare, with Sergeant MacLeod still padding back and forward between telephones on an overtime basis and only a couple of detective constables as a last reserve, both already busy.

A telephone call to the duty officer at Marine Division and a heavy reminder of past favours from Millside brought a promise that one of the Marine cars would help at the dockside. The plain-clothes team checking out the supermarket fire would have to get on with it on their own.

Thane dealt with the press conference next, ten minutes of parrying questions yet trying to keep the newsmen reasonably happy for practical reasons. Keep the press, radio and TV squads in a friendly mood and they could be useful in any murder hunt.

When that finished and the last reporter had left, he thumbed Sergeant MacLeod to come with him and went back into his own office.

'Sit down, Mac,' he said wearily, flopping down into his chair and leaning on the desk. 'For a minute, anyway – I've got work for you.'

'Sir?' The other chair creaked as MacLeod lowered his considerable bulk and waited with a cautious neutrality on his broad Highland face.

'Begin with Uniformed Branch,' Thane told him. 'Say we need every Peeping Tom complaint reported in the Division over the last couple of months. I don't care if they came in from hopeful old ladies or because someone didn't like the milkman, get them. As soon as you've got that started, contact Criminal Records. I want a rundown on all known sexual offenders we may have around Millside. The lot, Mac, from the downright petty through to rape.'

MacLeod grunted warily. 'How far back, sir? It could be quite a list.'

'I don't particularly want the dirty old men,' said Thane, accepting the sense behind MacLeod's query. 'We need the ones still young enough to run like hell – or to heave a girl into a car boot.'

'Fit funnies?' asked MacLeod frowning, already thinking of what would have to be done when the list came in.

'Yes.' Thane scribbled the Swanhill Street address on a piece of paper and passed it over. 'But before you do anything, scrape up a policewoman from somewhere and get her out to a girl called Jenny Fallon. Tell her I want everything the Fallon girl knows about Doreen Ashton.'

43

MacLeod left. A few minutes later an orderly came in with a large mug of tea from the brew the switchboard girls always kept going. By then, Thane had roughed out the preliminary report Headquarters wanted and gave it to the orderly to be sent over.

During the next half-hour his telephone rang several times. The only call that in any way mattered was from Phil Moss, to say he'd arrived down at the Spanish ship and everything was quiet again.

'How are things at your end?' asked Moss over the line.

'Grinding along, Phil,' said Thane, sipping the last of the tea in the mug and finding it had gone cold. 'Did you hear if the County cops made contact with Doreen Ashton's boss?'

'They did.' A mild cynicism entered Moss's voice. 'They say he made shocked noises but didn't exactly want to come rushing in. That was all.'

'He'll keep.' He told Moss to call it a day then hung up and glanced at his watch. It was nearly three a.m.

He dragged out the folding camp-bed from its cupboard, considered it with even more disgust than usual, then kicked off his shoes and loosened his tie. Any kind of sleep was better than none.

Bright sunshine streaming through the grimy window wakened Colin Thane before seven a.m. and he was using a battery razor at his desk, a tiny metal mirror propped against the telephone, when Phil Moss marched in.

'All yours and good morning.' Moss thumped a thick file of report sheets beside the mirror, yawned, scratched his scrawny stomach for a moment, then dragged a bundle of morning papers from his jacket pocket. 'Seen these?'

'Spread them out, Phil.' Thane finished shaving,

fastened his shirt, knotted his tie, then glanced wryly at the front pages. Doreen Aston's murder had made most of them in a big way – local killings always made better breakfast reading than distant disasters, industrial strikes or the cost of living.

'When do we let them have her name?' queried Moss.

'Lunchtime radio and TV bulletins and the evening papers is soon enough.' Thane lit his opening cigarette of the day, hated the taste, coughed through the first few draws of smoke, and began to feel awake. He thumbed at the report sheets. 'What about that lot?'

'I took a look – it's most of what you asked for, but we haven't dredged up anything wonderful.' Moss perched himself on the desk. 'In case you're interested, we've now got four Spaniards going through court for those knifings. Their ship is due to sail at the end of the week, but her captain says he hasn't enough crew without them.'

'That's his problem.' Thane began flicking his way through the report sheets. Plenty of people had been busy while he slept and now it was his turn again to pick up the threads and take over. Records Office had produced the list of known sexual offenders living in Millside Division. He raised an eyebrow at its length but tossed it towards Moss. 'Put a team to work checking them out, Phil – but gently.'

'Don't make waves.' Moss nodded, tucked the list away, then added greyly, 'It could be a waste of time. She was trying to contact us, remember?'

'Contact me, you mean.' Thane appreciated the early morning delicacy, but that also meant his second-in-command was troubled. He wondered how much sleep Moss had had overnight. At least he'd eaten – there were fresh stains on his stringy tie. 'There's always that Peeping Tom.'

'He's been around all right.' Leaning over, Moss extracted a Uniformed Branch memo sheet from the other reports. 'From this lot, he should have eye strain.'

Thane read the memo sheet and nodded a surprised agreement. The complaints were scattered in terms of time and place and were all minor, from the usual face at a bedroom window to the woman who had three pairs of panties stolen from a line of washing hung out overnight to dry. Normally it would have remained a Uniformed Branch problem with a low priority, but Millside certainly had at least one very active Tom on the prowl.

He abandoned the memo and picked up the next item from the collection. It was several close-typed pages thick – Probationer Constable Robby Deacon had been told to forget nothing in his report and it looked as though he'd obeyed to the last letter.

'We'll have Deacon in later, Phil,' he said absently, glancing quickly over the pages. The youngster's story didn't seem to fill in any significant gaps, though it included a list of all the car-club enthusiasts he'd known by name who'd been out on the rally preparation evening. 'This isn't bad for a rookie report.'

'So we pat him on the head?' asked Moss acidly. 'I don't like cops who know how to spell – that's not their business. And I don't like the way he was on his own, no alibi, till one a.m. That stinks.'

The telephone ringing saved Thane from having to reply. He picked up the receiver, answered, and heard an only-too-familiar voice rasping over the line.

'A nice sunny day for a murder inquiry, Thane.' Detective Chief Superintendent Buddha Ilford, head of the city's C.I.D. force, sounded almost amiable. But Ilford was probably still having breakfast and threw a different set of switches when he got to his desk. 'Why aren't you out in it – working?'

'We're starting, sir.' He saw Moss's raised eyebrow and nodded. Grinning, Moss came closer to eavesdrop. 'There's a preliminary report waiting on your desk.'

'I'd rather have you tell it, up-to-date. See me at Headquarters in an hour,' said Ilford shortly, and hung up.

Replacing his own receiver, Thane shrugged. 'You heard, Phil.'

'I'm glad he likes the weather,' said Moss dryly. 'That helps.'

'Till he decides it's too warm.' Thane stubbed his cigarette and took the last of the reports. It was handwritten and faintly perfumed. That meant Jean Donald had been the policewoman who'd gone to talk to Jenny Fallon. Jean had the kind of looks which made her automatic choice as bait in a set-up – but she also knew what was wanted. 'Now shut up. This one matters.'

Doreen Ashton, aged twenty-four, dark hair, blue eyes, height five feet seven, weight approximately one hundred and ten pounds, now a corpse with a tag round one ankle at the City Mortuary, had shared the basement apartment with her two companions for just over eighteen months. She'd no steady boyfriend apart from the Merchant Navy engineer, was easy-going in temperament and had no known money troubles.

'Pretty ordinary,' was Moss's brief verdict.

'Or it looks that way.' Thane slipped the report back with the rest and flicked the folder shut. There were tens of thousands of working girls like Doreen Ashton in any big city, leading ordinary, normal lives – and because they were ordinary and normal they were always the hardest from a cop's viewpoint when

47

something happened. 'You'd better check out the Merchant Navy angle.'

'Make sure the sailor really is at sea?' Moss grunted his understanding. 'What else?'

'Have another look at Deacon's car club list, then remind Doc Williams we're in a hurry for that post-mortem report.' Thane rose as he spoke. 'I'll check we've no more problems with those Spanish knife enthusiasts, grab some breakfast, then get over to Headquarters.'

'That leaves her boss,' reminded Moss.

'At his office,' nodded Thane. 'Duncan MacRath – well, he may have his own angle on the girl.'

'You've given him time enough to think one out,' said Moss acidly. 'If we'd got him last night –'

'We'd have known even less than we do now.' Thane grinned at him. 'Relax, Phil. Maybe he did give the Ashton girl a lift back to town, maybe he didn't. But either way, we've also given him time to worry.'

'Psychology next?' Moss looked disgusted but left it at that.

The driver on the Millside duty C.I.D. car was Erickson, a big, blond Viking of a man who was studying so that he could quit the force and become a lawyer. When Colin Thane joined him there was still time in hand before the appointment at Police Headquarters so he had Erickson drive round by way of Leyland Street.

'But don't stop,' he warned Erickson as the waste ground appeared ahead. 'I don't want to get involved right now.'

They drove past at a crawl. Several police vehicles were parked along the kerb, some of the Scientific Bureau men were again working at the abandoned Volvo, and a thin line of uniformed men had begun

48

combing their way through the weeds and rubble on the far side.

The free entertainment had produced an audience. A cluster of spectators, mostly women and children, lined the rope barrier which sealed off the area. Thane saw a woman with a pram among them, than another who was trying to hold up a small boy so that he could have a better view. As the car drew level, a round-faced young man in work overalls and wearing heavy spectacles took the child and held him higher.

'What the hell do they get out of it, sir?' asked Erickson bleakly as the duty car gathered speed again.

'A nice, second-hand touch of the horrors,' said Thane wryly, settling back. 'It's called human nature. Don't they teach you about that at law school?'

Erickson shrugged and lapsed into a gloomy silence.

The day was growing warmer by the minute as they neared the city centre, and the spring sunlight beamed down on a skyline few Glaswegians who had been away for any length of time would have recognized. After a horrendous period of reconstruction, which had reduced dozens of streets to bomb-site appearance, the commercial and business heart of Glasgow was taking on a new shape.

A few historic old landmarks had been preserved. But most of the rest was becoming a concrete and glass network of modern high-rise office blocks and shopping precincts.

Police Headquarters hadn't escaped in the process. A convoy of trucks had shifted all that was wanted from the old, worn-out block in St Andrew's Square to a new administration building in Pitt Street.

The Divisions called the new building Royal David's City – for reasons more associated with the name of the Chief Constable than anything Biblical. It housed the most modern police computer system in

Western Europe, which was also said to be good at forecasting race results. Visiting cops still stumbled lost and desperate through the corridors. But the first homely touches of obscene graffiti were already beginning to appear on the walls of its basement cells.

Only appearances changed.

'How long, sir?' asked Erickson as they pulled up at the main door.

'Fifteen, twenty minutes,' said Thane, getting out. 'Stay handy – and for Pete's sake don't get another parking ticket.'

Erickson grinned. The city's traffic wardens were campaigning for a wage increase and, in the process, were slapping tickets on anything with wheels that came within reach. It took time to square a parking ticket with their department, and they knew it.

'I could charge the baskets with loitering,' he said thoughtfully.

Deciding it sounded a good way to start a real war, Thane left him and went into the building. The new Headquarters still smelled that way, very different from the decades of stale sweat and disinfectant that had reigned in its previous home. Even the elevator which took him up to the top floor hadn't a scratch on its button panels and the door opened again with the softest of sighs.

Chief Superintendent William 'Buddha' Ilford's office was at the far end of the corridor. Thane knocked on the glass-panelled door then went in as the 'enter' signal lit up.

'You're on time.' Ilford, a bulky, balding man in a blue business suit, rumbled the greeting. He sat behind the battered desk he'd insisted on salvaging from his previous lair and considered Thane cynic-ally. 'That's usually a sign you don't know what else to do.'

'It's more a new approach I'm trying, sir,' answered Thane mildly.

Ilford grunted, signalled him to close the door and sit down, then spent a few moments using a kitchen match and one large thumb while he lit his favourite pipe.

'All right, I've read your first report again,' he said after the smoke had begun rising towards the acoustically tiled ceiling. 'That didn't involve any major intellectual effort. Now tell me the rest, man – briefly. I've things to do before the Chief Constable's meeting.'

Nodding, Thane quickly sketched through the general outline while Ilford listened in silence, puffing on the pipe, his head sunk down and his gaze contemplating his navel area in the way which had earned him the Buddha label.

'You're checking your sex offenders?' he asked as Thane finished.

'Yes.' Thane rubbed his chin warily. 'But we're not leaning on any of them.'

'Keep it that way.' Ilford sucked on his pipe again. 'Till you've got something definite in mind, at any rate. You said her shoes were missing – if they don't turn up, remember the fetish angle. Some of those characters like to keep souvenirs. I'll ask the computer what it thinks.'

'That might help,' said Thane cautiously. Ever since the computer had started working, Buddha Ilford had been like a child with a new toy. 'But we could be looking for someone she knew.'

'I hope you are,' said Ilford bleakly. 'Right now we can do without being landed with a wandering homicidal sex-maniac – I go off on leave next week.' He paused. 'You've still to talk to this rally-driver character MacRath, correct?'

'He's next on the list, sir.'

51

'I know his firm.' Ilford grinned a little behind the pipe. 'They do pretty well. I can tell you the Chief Constable knows his family too. Not that it makes a blind bit of difference – but it's worth remembering.'

'Sir?' Deliberately, Thane looked blank.

'Be your age,' said Ilford wearily. 'Just don't treat him like a ned.'

Glancing at his watch, Ilford removed his pipe from his mouth and knocked it out on the ashtray in front of him. Taking the hint, Thane rose.

'I'll keep in touch, sir,' he promised, heading for the door.

'That'll make a spectacular change,' said Ilford with a heavy sarcasm. Then, as the door closed, he heaved a sigh and reached for the papers he needed for the Chief Constable's meeting.

There were times when Buddha Ilford would have given a lot to be running a Divisional C.I.D. squad again, and to hell with the top-brass conferences. When the weather was good, at any rate.

The Glenrath Whisky Investment Corporation had its office in a commercial block in Bath Street, in the heart of the city's business area. The same block held a useful mix of accountants, lawyers and insurance firms and was the kind of address that didn't come cheaply.

Which left Phil Moss's shabby figure looking more than out of place as he waited at the pavement's edge. He brightened as the Millside duty car halted alongside him and Colin Thane got out.

'How'd it go with Buddha Ilford?' he asked as they met.

'He didn't exactly say we were wonderful,' admitted Thane wryly. 'And he's got a thing about shoes.'

'That's his age telling,' said Moss solemnly.

'You're always a help,' said Thane stonily. 'Has MacRath arrived yet?'

'Looks like it.' Moss nodded towards a parking bay across the street. It was occupied by a large Ford Capri Ghia in full rally trim. 'That was here when I arrived. How do we play it when we see him?'

'Straight,' said Thane shortly. 'Come on.'

Raising an eyebrow, Moss followed him into the building. The Glenrath office was on the third floor and small compared with some of its neighbours. At the inquiry counter, a young, long-haired clerk came over with a look of nervous anticipation while behind him the rest of the outer office staff, another clerk and a couple of typists, stopped any pretence at work and stared.

'Chief Inspector Thane,' said Thane mildly. 'Mr MacRath is expecting us.'

'He told us, Chief Inspector.' The clerk scratched at a pimple on his baby-smooth face without realizing it and swallowed. 'I – all of us got a real shake about Doreen. The papers didn't say it was her and –'

'Did you like her?' asked Moss casually.

'Yes.' The young face flushed. 'She was something special. If you'd seen her –' he stopped and winced – 'well, I suppose you did. But not here, I mean.'

He turned away, used an internal telephone briefly, then came back and led them through an inner door marked Private. It opened into a small hallway where he stopped at another door and knocked before opening it and standing back.

'Come in, Chief Inspector.' The man standing just inside the doorway was as tall as Thane, but younger, wiry in build and had black wavy hair and a strong face dominated by a positive eagle beak of a nose. He was in his shirt sleeves, a plain blue silk tie knotted loosely under an unbuttoned collar. 'I'm Duncan MacRath – and I can guess why you're here.'

53

As Thane and Moss entered the clerk closed the door behind them and vanished. Thane shook hands with MacRath, introduced Moss, then took a quick look around. Duncan MacRath's office didn't have a desk. Instead, a glass-topped circular table at coffee height was surrounded by several leather and chrome executive chairs. The walls around were covered in photographs of rally cars and a shelf above a long teak cabinet was lined with silver plaques and cups.

'Sit down, both of you. Cigarette?' As they settled, MacRath offered a silver cigarette box, then snapped a matching lighter for each of them in turn. He didn't take one himself, but chose a chair on the opposite side of the table and sat back, his hands building a miniature steeple under his chin with the fingertips barely touching. They were strong hands and long, powerful fingers, but they showed several minor scratches and abrasions.

'The County police called you last night,' began Thane.

'Right.' For a moment a flicker of anger showed in MacRath's brown eyes. 'After one a.m. Did I know a Doreen Ashton and, if I did, they were to tell me she'd been murdered in Glasgow. End – apart from adding that you'd be here this morning and what I read in the papers.' His mouth tightened. 'That's a pretty brutal way to do it, Chief Inspector. Or is that the usual drill?'

'We simply wanted to get word to you,' said Thane neutrally.

'You got it.' MacRath drew a deep breath. 'I want to know what happened last night. Doreen didn't just work here – she was a friend as far as I was concerned.'

'We had that notion,' murmured Moss blandly.

'Meaning?' The man switched his gaze and stiffened. 'Don't jump to too many conclusions, Inspector.

I want to help you, but when I say a friend I mean just that – no more.'

'You want to know what happened and so do we,' said Thane quietly. 'She was found dead on that vacant lot, hidden inside an old car. It could be someone jumped her and killed her when she fought back. But you're wrong if you think it happened last night. She'd been dead twenty-four hours by then.'

Duncan MacRath froze, looked at them both, then swore softly under his breath.

'She was with me the night before last,' he said slowly.

'At Drymen, helping on some car-rally route,' Thane agreed woodenly. 'We knew about that.'

'Did you know I also drove her home afterwards?' asked MacRath.

'We wondered,' said Thane, watching him.

'Well, I did – and I dropped her in Leyland Street, beside that waste ground.' MacRath chewed his lower lip hard for a moment, then shook his head. 'I read it had happened there, but I still didn't think –'

'Even though she didn't turn up for work yesterday?' queried Moss in a voice one stage short of open disbelief.

'Girls go off sick for the odd day and she hadn't been feeling too good.' MacRath stopped and got to his feet. 'Look, I'll tell you anything you want. But I think I'd like my brother Peter in here as some kind of a witness. He's just a couple of rooms away, and we shared Doreen as a secretary.'

Thane nodded and MacRath stalked out of the room. He was gone under a minute and when he came back the man who followed him in was a slightly younger edition. Peter MacRath, dressed in a dark blue business suit with a carefully knotted tie and a bright red edge of handkerchief showing in his top pocket, had the same strong features and wiry build as his brother. But he had fair hair and was a couple of inches smaller.

'Duncan's told me the score to date,' he said bleakly after minimal introductions. He glanced at his brother. 'Maybe we should get one of those lawyers on the next floor to take a wander down.'

'Stuff that,' said Duncan MacRath bluntly. 'You'll do for now.' He saw Moss had his notebook out and nodded. 'Go ahead, take notes if you want. I don't mind.'

'Then just tell us how it happened,' suggested Thane.

'Right.' Duncan MacRath slumped down in his chair again, gesturing Peter to do the same. 'I drove Doreen home and dropped her in Leyland Street. That would be – well, maybe about eleven o'clock that night.'

'Why Leyland Street?' asked Thane. 'Why not take her to her door?'

'Because Swanhill Street is a long way round by road from there,' said Duncan MacRath wearily. 'Hell, don't you think I wish I'd done that now? But any time I gave her a lift it was to Leyland Street, then she walked across to the other side. All the locals used the same shortcut.'

'I've driven her home a couple of times myself, when we've been working late,' volunteered Peter MacRath. 'She always said Leyland Street would do – she liked the walk from there.'

'There was one time I did go to her flat,' said Duncan MacRath heavily. 'I met the two girls she lived with and they seemed to get on well together. How are they taking this?'

'The way you'd expect.' Thane left it at that and leaned forward. 'Let's start again, at Drymen this time.'

Duncan MacRath helped himself to a cigarette from the silver box and lit it with a rock-steady hand before he replied.

'First, the reason we were there, the Forest Two Hundred Miles – that's a car rally, Chief Inspector. It rates as one of the biggest in the West of Scotland and it takes place this weekend. I'm driving in it –' he glanced round at the trophies behind him and smiled wryly – 'in fact, I won the damned thing last year.'

'We've another interest in the Forest Two Hundred,' interrupted Peter MacRath. 'The firm is putting up a trophy this time, the Glenrath Cup. It goes to the best novice driver.'

'Right,' agreed his brother. 'In fact, best bet to win it is Robby Deacon, a youngster who is training to be a cop.' He stopped, realization dawning. 'Deacon was at Drymen –'

'We've got his story,' said Moss easily.

'That must be useful,' said Duncan MacRath with a grim half-laugh that held no humour. 'Well, Deacon and I are both in the Strathclyde Car Club, which is running the rally. Normally, a competing driver doesn't help lay out a rally route, but the club needed all the help it could get this time. The Forest Two Hundred is a special sections event – more driving than navigation, so it was fair enough to be there.'

'Who took Doreen Ashton out to Drymen?' asked Thane.

'Some friends. We give each other lifts all the time.'

'I'd have expected someone who was a car enthusiast to have a car of her own,' frowned Moss. 'Didn't she drive?'

'Doreen could drive all right.' Peter MacRath took the question and gave a wry shrug. 'She joked around that she couldn't afford to own a car because we didn't pay her enough.' He paused, ran a hand over his fair hair, and glanced at his brother. 'But there was another reason.'

'She lost her driving licence about four years ago,' said Duncan MacRath wearily. 'She was driving, there was a crash, and the other driver was killed. A judge who didn't like women drivers kept her out of jail but banned her for five years. Doreen didn't like people to know about it, but she told us.'

'You drove her home from Drymen,' said Thane quietly. 'That's eighteen miles from Glasgow. You stay near Helensburgh. That's another twenty or so miles back out, isn't it?'

'So it meant maybe an extra forty minutes' driving,' shrugged MacRath. 'The people who brought her left early, then a few of us who worked on till it was dark went for a drink together. Hell, did you expect me to tell her to walk? We were back in town before eleven-thirty, I dropped her at Leyland Street, then I headed straight home from there.'

'You didn't wait to see her cross that waste ground at Leyland Street?'

'No.' It came like a sigh.

'Did you see anyone else there?'

'It was dark. Anyway, do you think I'd be sitting here like a paralysed monkey saying nothing if I had?' exploded MacRath.

'Easy,' murmured his brother. 'Easy, Duncan. They're only doing their job.'

'Then maybe they should be doing it some other damned place.' MacRath glared at them across the table.

'Believe it or not, you're still helping,' said Thane with a dry edge. He switched his attention to Peter MacRath. 'Do you remember your brother coming home?'

'Yes.' The fair head nodded emphatically.

'Like hell you do,' growled Duncan MacRath. 'You were snoring in your pit – everybody was. Even the bloody dog was asleep.'

'Then no,' said Peter MacRath sadly. 'But –'

'But nothing.' Duncan MacRath drew a deep breath. 'What next, Chief Inspector?'

Thane shrugged. 'You said she didn't seem too well that night. What did you mean?'

'She didn't say anything. She just wasn't as bright as usual – it was the same during the day, wasn't it, Pete?'

Peter MacRath nodded. 'Her typing had gone to hell too, and that was unusual.' He grimaced. 'I thought she maybe had 'flu coming on and said she should take a day off. That's why we didn't worry when she didn't show up yesterday.'

'It's understandable,' said Thane. It also fitted into the general background which was building around the dead girl. He signalled Moss, who tucked his notebook away, and added, 'While we're here, we'd better check her desk.'

The brothers glanced at each other and shrugged.

'Next door,' said Duncan MacRath, rising. 'I'll show you.'

'Phil –' Thane let Moss follow the man out. Then he stubbed out his cigarette on the big ashtray in the middle of the glass-topped table and twisted a grin at Peter MacRath. 'This part is never easy, believe me.'

'I got that feeling,' said MacRath, and grimaced apologetically. 'Duncan blows his top fairly regularly – except when he's driving.' He hesitated. 'Like a drink while you're waiting? We're more or less in the trade, so the whisky's pretty good.'

'Another time maybe.' Thane shook his head. 'Just what is your line here? Glenrath Whisky Investment doesn't exactly spell it out.'

Peter MacRath grinned. 'It's what it says – investment in whisky. Whisky has to mature for a minimum of five to seven years once it leaves a distillery, right? But there are plenty of small distilleries with cash-flow problems who sometimes can't wait that long for a return. So we're middlemen – we find people who want to invest money, long-term. We buy raw whisky for them, store it under bond, look after things, then arrange a buyer when the time comes round.'

'Does it beat the local savings bank?' asked Thane warily, in uncertain territory.

'Deduct our management fees, warehousing and tax and they can pick up a sizeable profit over the five years if the market's right,' said Peter MacRath cheerfully. 'Most of our clients seem happy enough. But it's a specialized line.'

'I believe you,' murmured Thane, whistling to himself.

'Our father ran the business till he died. Now three of us are in it – Duncan, myself and my mother.' Peter MacRath eyed him in an almost friendly way. 'We've got some clients who might surprise you.'

'Including one called Ilford?' guessed Thane, remembering the C.I.D. chief's interest.

'In a small way, yes. But I didn't tell you – our client list is confidential.' Peter MacRath winked, then turned as his brother entered the room again with Moss.

'Nothing,' said Moss shortly, shaking his head.

'I still don't know what the hell you hoped to find,' complained Duncan MacRath suspiciously.

'Neither do I,' said Moss acidly. 'But that's how it goes, Mr MacRath.'

'And we're finished for now,' said Thane, rising. 'But if we need help –'

'Come here or our house,' suggested Peter MacRath. 'Any time – right, Duncan?'

'I can't think of any way to stop them,' said Duncan MacRath with a minimal enthusiasm.

They left the two brothers and went back out through the main office. All activity there seemed to have come to a complete halt.

One way and another, it looked as if Glenrath's whisky investors wouldn't have much work done on their behalf for the rest of the day.

And that included Buddha Ilford.

Chapter Three

'What do you think?' asked Phil Moss as soon as they were back in the street.

'I'd give us ten out of ten for effort. Not much on results.' A tiny shoot of green tipped by a miniature blue flower was growing from a crack in the wall of the office block. Thane eyed it sadly. How it had got there was a minor miracle, how it survived among the traffic fumes a bigger one. 'He has a pretty weak story, but –'

'But they're the kind that usually stand up,' Moss finished for him as they walked towards the Millside car. 'Even without brother trying to help.'

'Families that stick together are getting scarce,' mused Thane. He had a notion that Duncan MacRath didn't go seeking favours from anyone. 'But Doreen Ashton still phoned us. If we knew why, it would make a difference.'

'Well, her desk didn't help.' Moss kicked a cigarette packet into the gutter with a scowl. 'She seems to have been the efficient type – a place for everything and everything in its damned place. And I can tell you something else that's in its place, the Merchant Navy boy friend.'

Thane raised an immediate eyebrow. 'For sure?'

'Positive,' declared Moss. 'An absolute check-out, Colin. John Abbott, second engineer on the tanker

Jerez Rose, present position approximately two hundred miles off Cape Town. The owners called me back just before I came here. They radioed the captain and he confirms Abbott is aboard.'

'Then he's out of the running. But there could be another boy friend around.' Reaching the car, Thane got in. As Moss followed, Thane leaned forward. 'All quiet, Erickson?'

'More or less, sir,' agreed Erickson laconically. He tossed the law book he'd been reading into the parcel shelf. 'Control radioed one message for you. Sergeant Easter at the Training Centre would like you to call in.'

Thane glanced at Moss with some surprise. The Easter Bunny didn't make contact for social reasons.

'We've got time,' he said slowly. 'Let's go there.'

The Millside car arrived at Oxford Street at the same time as a swarm of motor-cycle patrolmen were buzzing out on their machines. The motor-cycle patrols always used the Training Centre canteen as their coffee stall. As the last machine rasped away, Erickson parked the car in the courtyard and looked hopefully in the same direction.

'Go ahead,' invited Moss sourly. 'You're having a hard day, almost as if you were working. But make it a quick one.'

Erickson grinned and ambled off, leaving them to look for Sergeant Easter. They found the training sergeant round at the rear of the building, supervising an advanced intake class of rookies who were practising with a rescue stretcher. Another instructor was strapped aboard the stretcher and being lowered out of a second-storey window, but things weren't going right and the theoretical victim's language was Technicolor.

Easter saw them and came over with a hoarse, chuckling laugh.

63

'Charlie's having trouble,' he said, thumbing over his shoulder. 'First time, they tried to open the window with his head. This time they damned nearly strangled him with one of the ropes.'

'Third time lucky,' agreed Thane dryly, watching the wildly swaying stretcher. 'You could sell tickets for this kind of show. What else is troubling you, Sergeant?'

'Young Robby Deacon.' Easter's grin vanished and his hoarse voice thickened uneasily. 'I heard about him and last night, sir. Why the hell they let a kid like him loose on a beat on his own –'

'It happens sometimes,' interrupted Moss wearily. 'Easter, you didn't bring us out so you could yack like a Police Federation spokesman, did you?'

'No,' Easter shook his head slowly. 'It's just that – well, some of the lads on another of the intake classes were gossiping this morning. I heard something then, that's all. Maybe I should have forgotten about it.'

'But you didn't,' said Thane bluntly. 'So let's have it.'

'You've seen his car.' Easter chewed his lip a moment. 'It seems one of the other lads wanted to borrow it last night but Deacon said no, that he was going to need it.'

'Last night?' Thane had a momentary vision of the lanky, white-faced young constable and swore to himself. 'You're sure?'

The Easter Bunny nodded soberly. 'His story was he had to make a quick journey somewhere while he was supposed to be on beat duty. Deacon reckoned if he used the car he could do it without his section sergeant finding out.'

'Anything else?' asked Moss softly.

'No.' Easter drew a deep breath. 'Look, Mr Thane, he's a good enough lad. If –'

'We'll take care of it,' said Thane, cutting him short. 'Better get me his Training Centre background file, Sergeant.'

'Yes, sir.' Easter went off towards the office block, looking far from happy.

The rescue squad had got their instructor victim to the ground. He came struggling out of the stretcher straps, cursing fluently as he ordered them back into line.

'Deacon didn't mention anything about his car before,' said Moss thoughtfully as they watched.

'No.' Thane's thoughts were chill, going ahead on the long-shot possibilities. There had been a body concealed partway along Robby Deacon's beat. A body a killer might have planned to move to some safer place if circumstances hadn't decided otherwise. Circumstances like two boys playing with matches at the wrong time in a way that had to attract attention. 'Where is he now?'

'Back at Millside, waiting like you told him.' Moss's thin face was hard to read. 'For a rookie, he's getting to be a problem – if it even just stays that way.'

In a couple of minutes Sergeant Easter returned with Robby Deacon's background file. He handed it over almost reluctantly.

'He's a good lad, sir,' he began again.

'You said that before,' Thane told him more brutally than he meant. 'When's his intake due back here?'

Easter thought for a moment. 'This afternoon. Procedure in juvenile offences – one of the Probation Department people is giving the lecture.'

Thane thanked him and turned away, heading back towards the car. But Moss waited a moment.

'About that lecture, Sergeant,' he said conversationally. 'Don't wait for him if he doesn't show up.'

Then he hurried over to the car and got aboard. Erickson was already there, and as it purred away the rescue squad were assembling for another try with their stretcher. But this time one of the rookies was strapped in place.

The Training Centre file on Robby Deacon was already several pages thick, from his initial application to join the Glasgow force onward. Flicking through the sheets while the Millside car weaved its way back through the city traffic, Colin Thane could follow every step of his probationer progress.

At the beginning, like every applicant, Deacon had had to go along to a police station and be solemnly measured for height, recorded and authenticated at five foot ten and a half inches. Then he'd had to produce two referees on character and had chosen the family doctor and a clergyman.

Thane grinned and squirmed round a little to avoid the way the sun was glaring straight into his eyes. Doctors and clergymen seemed to spend more time certifying people as upright citizens than working at their regular professions. But at least they were usually reliable.

The next form was personal background. Single, aged twenty-two, Deacon came from a small mining town in Ayrshire. Since leaving school he'd been employed for a spell as a junior clerk in a bank then had gone from there to work as a salesman. He hadn't been a member of a trade union or a youth organization, he gave his outside interests as motor sport and swimming.

Then came the Recruiting Department summaries. The usual S.C.R.O. and Special Branch checks gave him a clean record. He had sailed through his medical and had scored 85 per cent on the educational tests. His personal interview rating was a rare 'excellent' and the confidential background inquiry, handled by a Headquarters sergeant, only revealed that he owed about two hundred pounds in future hire-purchase payments on his car.

The Millside car stopped at traffic lights and Thane looked up. They had crossed the river again and were at Argyle Street, with a flood of shoppers pouring from one pavement to the other. He ignored them, grimacing, thinking of the three hundred he owed on his own family car. Then there was Mary's new washing machine – he was glad to get back to the file as the lights changed and Erickson drove on.

The whole file told the same story. Even the most recent of the training reports, which began with an instructor's complaint that 'Probationer Constable Deacon continues to show too much independence of outlook', finished by giving him top rating in evidence presentation.

From references onward, Robby Deacon had all the apparent makings of a good cop, a well-above-average cop.

If he hadn't fouled things up now, one way or another.

He laid the file closed on his lap and sat back, eyes half-closed, conscious that Phil Moss had begun cleaning his fingernails with a rusty penknife. The car purred on, handled by Erickson with his usual lazy precision while the streets flickered past in a dusty, sunlit blur. Thinking came hard and came down to tenuous possibilities.

Suddenly – or it seemed suddenly – Moss's elbow nudged his side. Erickson was taking them back to Leyland Street and the stretch of waste ground lay ahead. The scene there reflected his own mood. Only a couple of police cars still remained with a few men standing near them and their audience had thinned to a handful of gapers.

He gave the spectators a casual glance, then his mouth tightened a little and he sat upright.

'Pull in, Erickson,' he ordered. 'But make it just past these people, not beside them.'

'What's up?' demanded Moss suspiciously as the car began to slow.

'Someone with a lot of time on his hands. Second from the left of that bunch,' said Thane softly.

It was the round-faced young man with the spectacles and work overalls. He had his hands in his pockets and for the moment was by himself.

'What about him?' demanded Moss as the car drew in and stopped, attracting a minor stir of interest.

'Just that he was hanging around when I passed this morning.' He ignored Moss's grunt of interest and switched his attention to the waiting group of police, seeking familiar faces, making his choice. It came down to the young, casually dressed figure of Detective Constable Beech, who still preserved the kind of brash innocence that got results, as it had with the Fortrose rent collector. 'Tell Beech to check him out. I'll give you some cover.'

They got out, Thane making noisy play at beckoning over the Uniformed Branch sergeant who was in charge of the group. As the sergeant came over, looking slightly peeved at being treated in that fashion, Moss strolled casually in Beech's direction.

'Any luck so far?' asked Thane as the sergeant reached him.

'No, sir.' The sergeant had a bloodstained handkerchief wrapped round a gash in his left hand. 'Unless you want to go into the junk business.'

'Then we'll have to try again, Sergeant,' declared Thane loudly. He added in a murmur, 'Play along with me. Keep it going.'

The sergeant raised one eyelid a tiny, surprised fraction but had sense enough not to ask questions. Solemnly, they crossed towards the derelict car and walked round it in apparent close conversation. The sergeant had a couple of planks of salvaged timber laid beside it. He'd found them dumped and wanted them to repair his garden shed.

Moss was back aboard the Millside car when Thane returned. The round-faced man with spectacles was still where they'd first seen him, but talking to an old woman with a shopping bag. Beech seemed to have vanished altogether, which meant he had started.

'He knows what to do,' said Moss briefly as their car drew away again.

Thane nodded and lit a cigarette. It might be a waste of time when Beech could have been better employed knocking doors with a routine checklist of questions. Yet chance always mattered, a hunch had to have its place in Colin Thane's calculations.

Particularly when anything approaching hard, positive fact was in short supply.

It was eleven a.m. when he entered the Millside office with Moss. At the public counter a small man who had a large Alsatian on a lead was making a noisy protest to the bar constable that whatever the neighbours said his dog wasn't dangerous. The Alsatian was doing its own spot of public relations, front paws resting on the counter top, but the bar constable was keeping well clear of its teeth. Behind them, a woman with a black eye was next in the queue.

Business as usual. A dog-eared poster on the wall behind the woman issued the hopeful invitation 'Join Scotland's Police – a Career with a Challenge.'

'Get Deacon and bring him up,' he told Moss. 'Make sure he hears on the way that we know about the car.'

Winking his understanding, Moss ambled off towards the muster-room area. Thane headed for the C.I.D. stairway but slowed as a voice hailed his name and an all-too-familiar figure headed towards him on a determined interception course. Chief Inspector Greystone was in charge of Millside's administration section. The whole division knew him better as the Olympic Flame because he never went out – of the office. Not if he could help it, anyway.

'What's wrong now?' asked Thane stonily. If a week passed without C.I.D. having a war with the Olympic Flame something unusual had occurred.

'Your Spaniards,' said Greystone with a scowl. He had a florid, beer-drinker's face, though he happened to be a rabid teetotaller. 'You'll need to do something about them, Thane.'

'Why?' He'd forgotten the seamen and their knives. 'Didn't they go through court this morning?'

'Yes.' Greystone gave a sniff. 'We got them straight back again on a two-day remand in custody for inquiry.'

'So?' It would have been more usual for the four to have drawn a four-day remand and been sent to the untried prisoner block at Barlinnie Prison, but it happened now and again. 'What's the problem?'

'Just that they started fighting again in the van coming back from court,' said Greystone bitterly. 'So they're in separate cells, Thane – four cells. I can't spare that kind of space. It means an accommodation problem.'

70

'You mean the locals might complain about over-crowding?' Thane saw not as much as a twinkle of a response from the Olympic Flame and sighed. 'I didn't get round to seeing the report. What's got them at each other's throats anyway?'

Greystone shrugged. 'Not my department.'

'Then let's find out,' said Thane curtly. He abandoned the stairway and swung down the corridor that led to the cell block, Greystone muttering at his heels.

Millside Division's cells were at the rear of the building. The floor was concrete, the walls tiled in yellowed white and the area always had a smell as stale as yesterday's dirty washing. The duty turnkey greeted Thane with a grin, greeted Greystone more cautiously and nodded wryly when their visit was explained.

'They're in the four cells on the left, sir,' he told Thane. 'No trouble now – but they were bawling the odds at each other for long enough even after we got them back.'

'Get them out,' ordered Thane. 'All of them.'

'Eh?' Greystone made a nervous throat-clearing protest. 'We don't want more trouble, Thane –'

'We won't have it,' Thane silenced him.

Shrugging, the turnkey opened the four cell doors in turn and thumbed the occupants out of their brick-and-tile cubicles. They emerged, looking around uncertainly then scowling at each other. Two sported white bandage dressings on their wounds, all were dressed in the seaman's off-duty rig of jeans and sweaters.

'Which of you speaks the best English?' asked Thane shortly.

The quartet switched their scowls in his direction, exchanged shrugs, then the smallest, who was bald

71

and had a bandage apparently holding one ear in place, eased forward.

'Me, *señor*.'

'You had an interpreter in court, right?' demanded Thane.

The seaman nodded.

'Then you know you're in trouble.'

The man gave an uneasy grin. '*Sí*. But our *capitán* says he cannot sail wit'out us, so –'

'So nothing,' snarled Thane. 'We've enough to do without you and your pals staging your own little private bull-fights every five minutes. Next time any of you as much as coughs without asking permission first we have a special place for him.' He raked his mind for the tourist Spanish that remained from a holiday years back. 'A place *muy mal* – not pleasant and comfortable like this. You understand?'

The bald man swallowed, looked around the cell block expressively then turned to his companions and spoke in a quick, low voice. They all looked uneasy by the time he'd finished.

'That's all,' barked Thane. 'Except one thing. What's the feud about?'

'A woman, I suppose,' sniffed Greystone. 'It usually is, with seamen.'

'No, *señor*,' protested the spokesman. He touched his bandaged ear warily but with a new indignation. 'Not a woman. This was more *importante* . . . football.' The word got home. His companions began muttering, slow-fuse style. 'Me an' my friend, we support Atletico Madrid – these other two say their team is better.'

'Football.' Thane raised an eyebrow. 'Who's the other Atletico fan?'

'Miguel.' The bald man indicated the seaman next to him then scowled at the others. 'These two support

Real Madrid – animals, *señor*. Uncultured animals.'

'We've a couple of football clubs here called Rangers and Celtic,' said Thane dryly. 'They've played your teams.'

'*Sí.*' The spokesman looked embarrassed. The matches concerned had been one stage short of open war, on and off the field. 'We – we remember, *señor*.'

'So do we.' Thane beckoned to the turnkey. 'Double them up – Atletico fans in one cell, Real supporters in the other.'

The turnkey obeyed. As the two cell doors slammed shut, Thane grinned at Greystone.

'Satisfied?' he asked. 'That saves you two cells.'

Greystone nodded reluctantly, then frowned. 'You threatened them. If their consul heard –' He stopped. 'What was that *muy mal* bit all about anyway?'

'I thought we'd maybe transfer them to work in your department,' said Thane mildly. 'That's the worst threat I can think of around here.'

The Olympic Flame was still spluttering as he left.

Back up in C.I.D. territory, Phil Moss still hadn't arrived with Deacon. That gave Colin Thane a chance to check the occurrence book, which had little fresh in it, and have a quick word with Sergeant MacLeod about the day-shift's dispersal before going through to the privacy of his own office.

Slumping down in the battered leather of the swivel chair he lit a cigarette, savoured the first draw of smoke from it, then had a look at the fresh paper which had arrived on his desk while he was out.

The door-to-door checks around Leyland Street had drawn a blank. Most of the Strathclyde Car Club members who'd been helping to prepare the rally section in the forest had been interviewed and their story tied in exactly with the versions he'd had from Robby Deacon and Duncan MacRath. A brief teleprinter message from Scientific Bureau confirmed what he'd been told earlier – they'd nothing to offer yet that could help. There was another message flimsy that Doc Williams would like him to call in at the City Mortuary after lunch.

He grimaced at that one. The police surgeon always got hungry when he was working on an autopsy. Though it still rang a faint warning bell – Doc's appetite for food was usually at its peak when things weren't too smooth.

Feeling hungry himself, Thane found another message slip almost lost beneath the rest. Mary had phoned twice. He had a slight pang of conscience, remembering that he hadn't been home. Mary was a cop's wife; she knew that was just part of the bargain, but they still had an unwritten agreement that one or other partner kept in touch.

Lifting the telephone, he dialled his home number and heard it ring out over the line. Then, cursing mildly, he hung up as he remembered it was Thursday. Mary always had lunch out with a girl friend on Thursdays.

Sitting back, he switched his thoughts to Doreen Ashton. It was now more than twelve hours since they'd found her body and he still wasn't much further forward than he'd been at the beginning.

So the only thing was to keep checking and trying. No matter how nebulous a particular line might seem. Opening the bottom drawer of his desk, Colin Thane dredged at the back among a bundle of old notebooks till he found the one he wanted. Each notebook held its quota of cases and contacts – the kind of contacts a detective collected along the way, to become part of his basic stock in trade.

He took out the notebook, flicked through its pages until he found the name he wanted, and folded an edge to mark the place as he heard a knock on the door.

The door opened and Robby Deacon came in first, followed by Moss. Closing the door again to shut out the sounds of the main office, Moss gave a slight nod.

'Sir.' Deacon was in uniform, his young face strained and slightly flushed. He came to a halt in front of Thane's desk, standing stiffly at attention with thumbs just touching his trouser side-seams in parade-ground style.

'At ease, Constable,' said Thane dispassionately. 'I want to talk to you again. I think you know why.'

Giving a sideways glance at Moss, the lanky probationer constable nodded. 'The car, sir.'

'Well?' Thane eyed him frostily. 'Where was it last night? Somewhere near Leyland Street?'

Deacon moistened his lips. 'Yes, sir. In – well, in a side-street about halfway along my beat. I didn't put that in my statement because –'

'Because you hoped we wouldn't find out,' Thane finished for him coldly. He leaned forward, one elbow on the desk, his eyes angry. 'What were you going to use it for, Deacon?'

'Something private, sir.' Deacon's voice was low and worried. 'But I didn't because – well, because of what happened.'

'Want us to feel sorry about that?' asked Moss cynically from the background. 'It must have been damned annoying, having a body dumped on your beat.' He shrugged in Thane's direction. 'Some people have no consideration.'

'None at all,' agreed Thane in a dangerously soft voice, his face impassive. 'All right, Deacon. You were going to sneak off from your beat for a spell. You

75

wouldn't be the first cop to do that. But I asked you already. Why?'

Deacon fingered the bright metal button of a tunic pocket and avoided meeting his gaze. 'Something personal, sir.'

'Personal, hell,' snapped Thane. He stabbed a forefinger in the younger man's direction. 'You saw that girl, Deacon. You knew her. In case you've forgotten, this happens to be a murder – for real, not some fun-and-games training school exercise for rookie cops. What were you going to do with that car?'

Deacon bit his lip but stayed silent. So Moss tried, almost sadly.

'Laddie, grow up. Hasn't it sunk into that thick skull of yours we're not talking about discipline codes?' He nodded slowly at Deacon's startled reaction. 'That's right. Your story checks out so far as it goes. But you say you were on your own when the girl was murdered – and that uniform you're wearing isn't an instant pass to being in the clear.'

Deacon's grip on the tunic button tightened until it seemed in danger of being pulled away. He swallowed hard and faced Thane again.

'I didn't think, sir. I –'

'Well?'

'It was the car, sir.' Deacon moistened his lips. 'I – there's the Forest Two Hundred coming up, and I'm getting her tuned. But I've got problems – I told you how I'd been working on her – and I know an all-night service station with an electronic test rig I can use. I thought if I had half an hour there –' He stopped, seeing Thane's expression, and protested, 'I've been short of time, sir. I just thought I could fiddle half an hour or so off. But it didn't happen.'

'Where is this service station?' asked Thane grimly.

'The Newfield Garage at Garrick Street, sir – you can ask them about me.'

'We will.' Thane's mouth tightened, every instinct telling him Deacon was lying. 'For now, you're suspended from normal duty. You can attend training-school classes, nothing more. Understood?'

'Sir.' Deacon flushed and stiffened again.

'That's all.' Thane sat stonily while the lanky figure turned disconsolately and went out. Then, as the door closed again, he swore softly and sat back.

'Believe him?' asked Moss dryly. 'I didn't.'

'I wouldn't bet either way.' Thane rummaged through the report sheets on his desk, found Deacon's statement, and pushed it over. 'Phil, have every line of this checked out again – and his story about the garage.'

'Right.' Moss gave a sympathetic belch. 'Are we eating in?'

Thane nodded and said nothing. Grimacing, Moss picked up the statement and left.

For a couple of minutes Colin Thane sat as he was, hearing the muffled street sounds outside, conscious of the sunlight streaming in, but his mind on Deacon. Then, at last, he shrugged and reached for the note-book in front of him.

He opened it at the page he'd marked and smiled slightly at the name and telephone number scribbled on the bottom line. John Kelso was a Surveyor of Customs and Excise, a Government tax-hound whose speciality was the whisky trade. The last time they'd met had been a couple of years before, and there were good reasons why neither of them should forget it.

Lighting a fresh cigarette, Thane lifted his telephone and dialled the Customs man's number. The switch-board girl who answered kept him waiting a few moments then Kelso's mild, warm voice came on the line. They spent a couple of minutes exchanging mutual greetings, then Thane switched his manner.

'John, I need some help.'

'I didn't think it would be a social call,' said Kelso wryly. 'What's your problem?'

'Some background – nothing else right now. Anything you know about an outfit called the Glenrath Whisky Investment Corporation.'

There was a pause on the line, then a cautious chuckle.

'The MacRath brothers?' Kelso didn't hide his curiosity. 'Have they been collecting too many parking tickets?'

'Just tell me how they rate,' countered Thane.

'Well, fine as far as we're concerned.' Kelso sounded slightly peeved. 'They store their clients' whisky in Government bonded warehouses, they pay the usual duty on the stuff when it comes out of bond – and their cheques don't bounce. It's a solid family business. Ah – met mother MacRath yet?'

'No.'

'Ah.' Kelso chuckled at the prospect. 'That's an experience. Victoria MacRath is a lady – and stainless steel in a lace glove. Those boys are her babies. She refused to sell the Glenrath outfit when her husband died, bossed it for a spell before she let the boys take over, and what she says still matters. Annoy her, and she'll singe your tail feathers.'

'Thanks for the warning,' responded Thane gloomily. 'I've got Duncan MacRath on the fringe of a murder– his secretary is the girl who was found at Leyland Street last night.'

'I read the story.' Kelso perked up. 'You mean you think –'

'I think nothing. I'm floundering around. I just want you to keep your ears open.'

'We usually do that anyway,' countered Kelso, then relented. 'All right, but watch out for widowed mother. She'll expect you to use the tradesman's entrance.'

'I'll practise my curtsy,' said Thane grimly, thanked him and hung up.

The call hadn't got him very far, but at least it was another aspect being watched, added to the rest from Peeping Toms to – he paused in the thought, then reluctantly added young Deacon.

Phil Moss barged in a moment later and slapped a package of sandwiches on the desk.

'Lunch,' he declared unenthusiastically. 'Take your pick – cheese or corned beef. Mac's finding some coffee.'

Sergeant MacLeod brought a couple of mugs of coffee soon afterwards, hung around for a little making sad noises about the amount of overtime he was clocking up, then went back out to the main office.

Finishing one sandwich, Thane flicked a crumb of corned beef from one of the report sheets, succeeded in smearing the paper in the process, and was reaching for another of the sandwiches when the telephone rang.

'I'll get it,' volunteered Moss through a mouthful of bread. He scooped up the receiver, grunted a greeting to the caller, listened for a moment, then chewed quickly and swallowed the food down.

'Say that again,' he demanded.

The voice at the other end obliged.

'Hold on.' Moss removed the receiver from his ear and turned to Thane. 'Colin, it's Beech. He's got what you wanted on that character you told him to tail from Leyland Street.'

Thane looked at the fresh sandwich in his hand then put it down. 'Well?'

'You might have something. His name is Harold Savoy, he lives on his own a couple of streets away from Doreen Ashton's apartment, and he hasn't been there more than three months.' Moss shaped a crooked grin. 'Didn't those Peeping Tom reports start about that time?'

'Yes.' Thane's interest quickened. 'What else has he got?'

'I'll ask.' Moss did, listened again, and gave a grunt of satisfaction before he switched his attention back to Thane. 'The neighbours reckon Savoy's a fairly odd character. He's friendly enough but never has visitors – as far as they know, no one has ever been inside his place since he arrived. And he goes out most nights.'

Thane located the sexual offenders list they'd got from Records and skimmed down the names. Harold Savoy wasn't among them, but he'd asked for a list of known offenders in the Millside area and if Savoy was a newcomer – he took the phone from Moss.

'Beech, where is he now?' he demanded.

'Gone off to work, I think, sir,' replied Beech cheerfully. 'I followed him back home, and he left again after a few minutes. I had to let him go so I could try the neighbours. But they say he's usually back about four in the afternoon.'

'Where does he work?'

Beech chuckled. 'He's a self-employed window cleaner, sir. With his own ladder. It sort of ties in, doesn't it? I mean, if he gets his specs steamed up by day –'

'The funnies can wait,' said Thane, an ancient, bawdy limerick about an old window cleaner called Adder who had a terrible fall off his ladder wisping through his mind. 'Stay around. Find out anything more you can without getting the neighbours too uptight and call me as soon as Savoy gets back.'

He hung up, buzzed Sergeant MacLeod on the desk intercom, and told him to contact Records Office at Headquarters for anything they had on a Harry Savoy. When he clicked the switch off and looked up, he found Phil Moss rubbing his bony hands almost happily.

'Maybe we've got something now,' said Moss hopefully.

Thane nodded. At least it was worth a positive check, and that was more than they had in other directions, even including Robby Deacon.

The telephone rang again before Moss could say more. Swearing mildly, Thane answered it then winced a little as Buddha Ilford's voice boomed in his ear. The city C.I.D. chief had a firm conviction that telephones were meant for shouting, no matter the distance involved.

'Keeping in touch, Thane, that's all,' said Ilford with an unusual heartiness. 'Anything fresh on your murder so far? The – ah – Chief Constable is expressing an interest.'

'For any particular reason, sir?' asked Thane innocently, grimacing at Moss. 'If it's the Glenrath firm, I've heard one or two people may have interests there –'

'Well – uh – perhaps some have.' For a moment, Ilford seemed caught off guard. Then he recovered. 'It makes good sense for a Scot to invest in a solid Scottish family firm, doesn't it?'

'If you've money to spare,' agreed Thane woodenly, then decided he'd better not prolong it. 'No, there's nothing really strong in any direction, except for a possible lead on the Peeping Tom angle.'

'That sounds as probable as any – these people can blow their tops occasionally.' Ilford made a throat-clearing noise. 'Still, if you do get involved

81

with the MacRath family you'd better know about their mother, Victoria MacRath.'

'I've already heard she's fairly iron-clad,' said Thane mildly.

'Then you've heard right,' answered Ilford almost wryly. 'If you meet the lady, treat her like you're walking on eggs – and hide Moss or she'll have him wash his neck. Victoria MacRath treats anything in trousers like they were five-year-olds.'

'I'll remember,' promised Thane. He hung up again as Ilford said goodbye, and this time found Moss frowning.

'What was that he said about me?' asked Moss indignantly.

'That I've to take you with me if we're contacting mother MacRath,' said Thane mildly. 'He thinks you two might hit it off together.'

'Women?' grunted Moss. 'I'd rather have steak and chips.'

And he helped himself to the last of the cheese sandwiches, which was already curling at the edges.

Criminal Records took fifteen minutes before they called back. But it was worth the wait. They had Harry 'Parrot' Savoy on file, last known address in the Eastern Division. Aged thirty, he had two previous convictions – one for indecent exposure several years back, when he'd been given the option of a fine by an intrigued lady magistrate, the other a three-month prison term for accosting schoolgirls. His photograph and record, added the bored voice at the other end of the line, were now on their way to Millside Division.

The package arrived within another quarter hour. Thane opened it, took one look at the broad, bespectacled face on the Records Office picture, and was satisfied.

'Do we pick him up?' asked Moss.

'Not yet.' Thane considered the photograph again. 'We'll wait till he gets home and do it the easy way. Phil, you stay with the Robby Deacon side – just in case. Then do some more asking around about the MacRath brothers. Both of them.'

Moss sniffed gloomily, but nodded. 'What about you?'

'Doreen Ashton's apartment again.' Stuffing the photograph in his pocket, Thane rose to his feet. 'I want to give that place another going-over.'

'Back to her telephone call again?' Moss understood and felt the same way. 'Hell, if she'd only given some kind of hint about what she wanted –'

'She didn't.' Thane reached the door, opened it, then glanced back. 'Meet up with me at the City Mortuary in an hour or so, Phil.'

'Why there?' asked Moss peevishly. 'They brew hellish coffee – the worst in town.'

'Doc Williams is making noises,' said Thane bleakly. 'We'd better find out why.'

It was three o'clock in the afternoon, the sky cloudy for a change and a gusty wind blowing the day's litter along the pavements, when the Millside duty car stopped at the kerb beside the basement apartment in Swanhill Street. A group of youths standing outside a corner grocery store watched with interest as Thane got out, but they stayed where they were. The grocery store took bets for the local bookmaker, and most of them had money on the three o'clock race.

The little blue and white basement door was opened for him by a policewoman who gave him a smile and a nod as he entered.

'How are things?' he asked.

'Reasonable I think, sir.' She glanced over his shoulder into the apartment, 'I only took over as relief at noon, but they're both friendly enough –'

'Both?' He raised an eyebrow.

'The other girl flew back from Ireland and got here about lunchtime, sir.' She closed the door and waited. 'Anything I can help with?'

'I'll talk to them first. Then we'll toothcomb through Doreen Ashton's room again.' He saw the question coming and shook his head. 'I won't know what I'm looking for till I find it.'

Jenny Fallon was sitting in one of the bean-bag chairs in the front room. She wore slacks and a sweater and her plump face managed a welcome smile as she saw him.

'I hear you've got company again,' said Thane.

She nodded, brushed a wisp of fair hair back from her forehead as she rose, and went over to the hall doorway.

'Mandy –' She called the name, then turned. 'The policewoman you sent last night managed to contact Mandy. She came back on the first plane she could get. I – well, your people have been good, Chief Inspector.'

'The friendly fuzz.' Thane smiled to put her at ease, then switched his gaze to the other girl who came in.

Mandy Ryan was tall, slim, had her dark hair cut even shorter than he'd seen in the photograph the night before, and was also in slacks and a sweater. As Jenny Fallon completed the introductions, her flat-mate addressed him in a voice which didn't try to hide its Irish accent.

84

'Was it this Peeping Tom character, Chief Inspector? Jenny said –'

'We don't know yet,' he stopped her. 'It takes time. When something does happen, you'll hear.'

Her mouth tightened. 'We want that, Chief Inspector. The three of us here – we were all good friends. With three girls sharing a flat, that's something special, believe me. Most times, put three like us –' she hesitated rather than stopped – 'like we were, I suppose it is now. Put three together, anyway, and they'll end up fighting like cats. But it didn't happen. Not with us.'

Jenny Fallon nodded agreement at her side. 'So if there's any way we can help, just say.'

'There might be.' He brought out the photograph of Harry Savoy. 'Take a look at this man. Ever seen him before, anywhere?'

They frowned over the photograph and exchanged a puzzled glance. Then Mandy Ryan nodded, still puzzled.

'That's our window-cleaner. He's a harmless lump of a man.' She looked at Thane's face. 'Well, isn't he?'

Thane shook his head and answered her with another question.

'How well do you know him?'

'The same as we know ..e postman or the milkboy, I suppose,' said Jenny Fallon uneasily. 'I don't even know his name. He just told us to call him Parrot.'

'That's right. It's some joke he has about how he perches on ladders.' Mandy Ryan moistened her lips a little and eyed Thane wisely. 'What else does he maybe perch on, Chief Inspector? Bedroom window-sills late at night?'

He shrugged. 'It's possible. But that's what I've got to ask you. Could Parrot be your Peeping Tom?'

'He does have the same kind of build,' agreed Mandy Ryan reluctantly. She gave a slight shiver of disgust. 'It's a sick kind of thing to even think about.'

They couldn't help him further. Telling them what he was going to do, he collected the policewoman and went through to Doreen Ashton's bedroom.

It was a small, cheerful little room, simply furnished and spotlessly clean, with a single window which looked out on to steps leading up to a backyard. The dressing table had a couple of crumpled cleansing tissues lying beside some jars of make-up, a discarded blouse was draped neatly over a chair, and the whole air gave the impression that Doreen Ashton might walk back into the room at any minute.

Except that she wouldn't, and they had a job to do. He took the dressing table, signalling the policewoman to deal with the clothing hanging in the wardrobe. Removing one drawer at a time, he emptied their contents on the bed. Underwear and tights, more make-up, a jewellery box and a bundle of letters with foreign stamps tumbled down. The letters were from the Merchant Navy boy friend, the jewellery amounted to a few inexpensive rings and brooches.

The policewoman drew a blank at the wardrobe. Thane left her to repack the dressing-table drawers and switched his attention to a suitcase he found under the bed. It held winter clothes, carefully packed away for another year. He left them littered on the floor and moved on to a small bookshelf mounted on the wall near the window.

The bookshelf held a crammed collection of oddments, but only a few books. Thane hauled them down, and some snapshot photographs spilled from the pages of *Motor Sport Yearbook*. He stooped, picked up the photographs, then frowned at one.

It showed Robby Deacon beside his battered Mini, with his arm round Doreen Ashton's waist. She had an arm round his neck, and both were laughing.

Putting the photograph to one side, he replaced the rest.

It took another fifteen minutes to complete the search and at the end the photograph was all he took when he left.

Mandy Ryan and Jenny Fallon were still in the front room and were talking quietly and earnestly together as he entered. They fell silent, glanced at each other, then Mandy Ryan came towards him.

'We want to ask you about that policewoman,' she said in a determined voice. 'Do we have to have her around now both of us are here?'

'No.' He felt amused at her resolute air. 'Why? Does she worry you?'

'She's all right,' frowned the dark-haired girl. 'But – well, we'd rather get used to what's happened on our own.'

'She's a stranger,' added Jenny Fallon more nervously. 'I know she means well, but –'

'She doesn't need to stay,' Thane assured them. 'In fact, we're pretty well finished here.'

'Good.' Mandy Ryan looked relieved then considered him oddly. 'Jenny says you asked her if Doreen had been acting worried about anything.'

'That's right.' He waited, deciding that if any decision had to be made between these two then Mandy Ryan was the dominant figure.

'I don't understand.' The girl's eyes were puzzled. 'I thought – well, that if there was anything, you'd know already.'

'Why?' Thane couldn't hide his surprise.

'Because I gave her your name.' Mandy Ryan gestured vaguely. 'It was just before I left on holiday. I thought –'

'Whatever you thought, you'd better tell me,' said Thane grimly. 'Starting with when this was.'

'A week ago – exactly a week ago tonight, because I was washing my hair.' She seemed to feel the logic was self-explanatory. 'Doreen came in and started talking. She said a friend had a problem and wanted to talk to someone in the police, someone semi-intelligent who would listen.'

'And you gave her my name?' Thane raised an eyebrow.

'I work in a lawyer's office,' said Mandy Ryan wearily. 'We're local, and we handle a lot of court work. I asked my boss the next day and he gave me your name – then I told Doreen.'

'Did you think she was really asking for a friend?'

The girl gave him a pitying look. 'Chief Inspector, we had rules –'

'You didn't ask questions,' he agreed caustically. 'Right now, that doesn't exactly help.'

'But Doreen didn't contact you?' chipped in Jenny Fallon.

'She didn't speak to me,' said Thane briefly.

But his thoughts were bitter as he left them.

Chapter Four

A squad of men with pneumatic drills were digging a hole in the road outside the City Mortuary. The staccato clatter of the drills and the rumble of the compressor penetrated through the red brick walls, along the tiled corridors, and even vibrated a glass specimen jug with a few wilted flowers which some house-proud attendant had placed on the table in the little office next to the autopsy room.

'I should get a hardship allowance,' complained Doc Williams. Seated behind the table, his slim, strong hands wrapped round a mug of coffee, he wore green overalls and white rubber boots. A pair of discarded rubber gloves lay in the waste-basket beside him. 'How would you like to try to hold a scalpel steady in this din?'

'I've no ambitions that way, Doc.' Straddling a chair saddle-style on the opposite side of the table, Colin Thane tasted his own coffee and grimaced. Mortuary coffee really was about the worst in Glasgow – and Moss had refused to even try it again. Instead, he was sitting back in another chair, eyes half-closed, apparently one stage short of yawning. 'Did you bring us here so you could lodge a protest?'

'No.' Doc Williams grinned wryly. 'I'd be happier if it had been. Colin, we've got problems with this girl.'

'What kind of problems?' asked Thane. 'Last night you said –'

'Forget what I said.' The police surgeon took a pencil and used it to stir his coffee. 'Last night we found a girl, she looked like she'd been strangled, she had marks on her body, her clothes were torn – it all looked like a rape that went wrong. Now, I don't know.'

Outside, the road drills yammered again and a few petals fell from the flowers in the jar.

'What don't you know?' Thane asked.

Doc Williams shrugged and waited for a moment till the drills died down again.

'It's a lot easier to tell you what I'm sure about,' he said almost apologetically. 'None of her injuries were caused while she was alive.'

Moss sat up straight and gave a mild belch of surprise.

'You know what you're saying?' he demanded with the tone of a man who doubted it.

'Yes.' Doc Williams nodded sadly. 'What we've got are injuries to the deep tissues of the throat appropriate to strangulation – even the hyoid bone was fractured, which is usually conclusive. But everything goes wrong after that.'

'I'd like it in plain language, Doc,' said Thane slowly, baffled.

'That isn't easy.' The police surgeon frowned at his own inadequacy. 'Post-mortem examination should have shown haemorrhage, capillary injuries, in the brain and the lungs and the heart muscle – it didn't. The skin colour isn't right, the whites of her eyes aren't right. Even the abrasions on her legs aren't right.' The frown became a scowl. 'Hell, do you want a lecture on it all? I'm telling you she was strangled after she was dead. That should be enough.'

'And you know damned well it isn't,' said Thane tightly. 'What did kill her?'

90

Doc Williams shrugged ruefully. 'Right now, I can't tell you. Anything from sheer fright onward – the thing is wide open.'

'Thanks,' said Thane bitterly. He got to his feet and crossed to a bench by the window where Doreen Ashton's clothes lay in a bundle, topped by a plastic bag containing the few personal items that had been found in her pockets. He picked up the scorched and torn remains of the white anorak jacket the girl had been wearing then threw it down again. 'All right, what are you doing about it?'

'Asking for help,' said Doc Williams simply and sadly. 'I've sent a parcel of tissue slides and organic specimens along to the Forensic Medicine Department at Glasgow University. Maybe their laboratory mob will come up with an answer.'

Thane nodded slowly. There was no love lost between Doc Williams and Professor MacMaster, the elderly tyrant who ran the university department. When the police surgeon asked for help from that direction it meant he really had problems.

'How long will it take, Doc?' asked Moss, ambling over to join Thane at the little heap of clothing.

'Maybe hours, maybe days.' Doc Williams watched as Thane opened the plastic bag and took out its contents. There was a purse with some small change, a little make-up bag with a pocket comb, lipstick and powder, cigarettes, a ball-point pen and, last of all, a couple of folded, crumpled sheets of printed paper.

Thane unfolded the paper. The two sheets were the Strathclyde Car Club's briefing to helpers on the Drymen rally section party, from the time they were to report to a cheerful footnote that anyone interested should bring their own beer.

'She travelled light,' mused Moss.

'Just the basics. It was that kind of outing.' Thane considered the bundle of clothing again. An anorak over a mini dress – most women faced with an evening's work in the open would have settled for trousers. But maybe Doreen Ashton had had other reasons. The thought sparked another. 'Can we even be sure she was killed on that waste ground?'

'No. Just that she died about twenty-four hours before your rookie cop found her.'

Moss began examining the anorak jacket. The pockets had been emptied in the usual way, by turning them inside out – all except a narrow pen-pocket high on the right side. Exploring it with a finger, he gave a sudden grunt, tried again, then fished out a small slip of paper. Smoothing the slip, he gave a soft whistle and passed it to Thane.

'Found something?' asked Doc Williams. He saw Thane's expression and came over. 'What is it?'

The slip appeared to have been torn from a notepad. Written on it in ink was 'Chief Inspector Thane, 1113'. Then, beneath, almost as an afterthought, the figures '2161'.

Doc Williams blinked. 'What the hell –'

'We knew she'd been trying to contact me,' said Thane bleakly.

Now they had final proof. Add the exchange dialling code, and 1113 was Millside Division's telephone number. But that left the other set.

'It could be another phone number,' suggested Moss. 'We can check the city exchanges.'

As if agreeing, the telephone on Doc Williams' desk began ringing. On cue, the pneumatic drills outside resumed their clatter.

Swearing, Moss answered the telephone, listened with a hand against his other ear, then snarled a request for the voice on the line to try again. This time he heard enough and turned to Thane.

'It's Beech. Our window-cleaning friend is back home and he wants to know what to do about it.'

'Tell him we'll be right over,' said Thane.

Leaving Moss to pass the message, he folded the slip of paper and put it in his wallet beside the photograph of Robby Deacon and Doreen Ashton.

His mouth tightened. Doreen Ashton was now just one more clinically dissected corpse, still lying on the glinting steel autopsy table in the next room.

But when she had scribbled on that slip of paper she had been someone who wanted his help – and that was something he couldn't forget.

For once, traffic was light in the city and the Millside duty car hardly slowed on the journey back to the division. Erickson was humming to himself behind the wheel and the only sound coming over the radio was an indignant squawking from Control. They were trying to raise a mobile to cope with a road accident on the south side and there were no takers.

'About those numbers,' said Moss suddenly. 'If 2161 isn't a telephone it could be a bank account or –'

'Or anything.'

'I'll still take it on.' Moss gave a fractional grin. 'I'd say it's more my territory – you're not the crossword-puzzle type.'

Thane nodded reluctantly, knowing he was right but still feeling that in the process he was parting with something tangible.

'Settled.' Moss produced a crumpled pack of cigarettes and gave him one before helping himself. Both had to be straightened before they could be lit. 'How did you get on at the girl's flat?'

Thane told him and Moss gave a soft, smoke-laced whistle when he heard about the photograph of Deacon with Doreen Ashton.

'Our rookie again?' He shook his head and watched the shop windows they were passing for a moment.

'Well, his story stays weak. They know him at the Newfield service station, but they didn't expect him to be along last night.'

It was no surprise. Thane glanced at his watch as the car stopped at traffic lights. Another couple of minutes should take them to Parrot Savoy's home.

'What about the MacRath brothers, Phil?'

'I've talked to some of the trade,' said Moss dryly. 'All I get is this line about a "solid family business" – or that Duncan drives like he was born on wheels. Peter is sort of overshadowed by Duncan. Though he has hidden talents of his own – like me.'

'Since when did you keep anything hidden, except your money?' asked Thane sardonically.

Moss looked hurt. 'When I was a kid at school I got the class vote as the boy most likely to succeed.'

'Then you became a cop – that was your big mistake.' Thane heard a chuckle up front and glared at the back of Erickson's neck. 'And when I want outside comments I'll ask for them.'

'Sir.' Erickson's eyes met his own innocently through the driving mirror. 'I was just thinking –'

'You, thinking?' Moss cut him short. 'Erickson, that's a delusion of grandeur – like your notion of becoming a whizz-kid lawyer. And if you ever make it, don't expect me to come knocking at your door – I'd rather take advice from a tame gorilla.'

Satisfied that he'd scored, he allowed himself another stomach tablet.

Harry 'Parrot' Savoy's address was a red sandstone terrace block in Ternhead Street, less than a five-minute walk away from where Doreen Ashton's body had been found. The Millside car drew in close by and as Thane and Moss got out they saw Detective Constable Beech emerge from the shadow of a doorway opposite. Beech came over quickly and confidently, smoothing down his wind-ruffled red hair as he reached them.

'He's still here, sir,' he reported briskly. 'Second floor, this entrance – I saw him at the window a couple of minutes ago, and he'd changed out of his work clothes. Uh – what's the score anyway?'

'You can come and find out,' said Thane shortly. 'We'll need your notebook.'

Obediently, Beech followed them into the block and up the stone stairway until they reached the second floor. There were four doors on the landing, all equally drab and in need of paint, and Beech gestured towards the second from the end. Thane rang the doorbell, they heard a soft double-chime, then, after a moment or two, there was the click of a heavy lock being turned and the door opened.

'Yes?' Parrot Savoy peered at them through the gap, his voice sharp and suspicious.

'Police.' Thane pushed his warrant card close to the man's horn-rimmed spectacles. 'We want to talk to you, Mr Savoy.'

The man's eyes widened for an instant behind the lenses and he moistened his fleshy lips. 'I don't know. I –' He looked down, saw Thane's foot firmly in the gap of the door and changed his protest to a shrug.

The door opened wider and they went into a small hallway with dingy white walls and a strip of old carpet on the floor. Closing the door again, the man faced them. Medium height and broad in build, Parrot Savoy was in grey cord slacks and a white, open-necked shirt. The sleeves were rolled up, showing hairy, muscular forearms, and his thinning fair hair, cut short, was carefully combed to cover a bald patch.

The word for him, decided Thane, was ordinary. Except when he spoke again, fast and with a forced indignation which reached a near squawk. Suddenly, Parrot Savoy's nickname made considerable sense.

'What's it about?' he demanded, his eyes darting round their faces. 'Look, I'm a busy man an' I've things to do. Important things, so–'

'So we'll get right down to it.' Thane looked over his shoulder into a small living room with faded furniture and a table which still bore the remains of a meal. 'In here?'

He didn't wait for an answer but led the way through and dropped down into one of the armchairs placed beside an unlit gas fire. Beech stayed by the door while Moss wandered over past the table and propped himself against the wall by a window.

'Well?' Parrot Savoy stood beside the other arm-chair, looked down at Thane and swallowed hard. 'I said what's it all about, eh? I mean, folk like you can't jus' come forcin' their way in –'

'As I remember it, you invited us, Parrot,' said Thane and saw Savoy's face twitch at the nickname. 'How's business in the window-cleaning game? Doing all right?'

'No complaints – till now.' It came as a mumble then Savoy's voice returned to a forced, nervous squawk. 'Look, I'm licensed, I pay taxes an' I don't owe money. What's more, I don't let folk push me around, mister. So don't think you can start har-assin' me.'

'Bull,' said Moss from his position near the window. His thin face shaped a cold grin as the spectacles jerked in his direction. 'Get off your perch, Parrot. Tell us how a convicted Peeping Tom conned his way into a window-cleaning licence.'

The man jerked as if he'd been stung, shot a glance at Beech who was giving an impression of wooden-faced innocence, then swung back to Thane.

'What do you want?' he asked hoarsely.

'A talk, like I told you.' Thane considered him stonily. 'We think you've been up to your old tricks again, Parrot.'

'Me?' Savoy backed a couple of steps away, shaking his head quickly. 'No – not since I did that three-month stretch in Barlinnie.'

'How was it there?' asked Thane mildly.

'God-awful.' Even the memory sent a near-shudder through the man. 'The screws, an' those cells – an' the stink. I nearly went crazy.' He spread his broad hands appealingly. 'Look, mister, maybe I take a walk now an' again at night. But that's just exercise – for the fresh air, like.'

'Keep-fit style?' Thane's voice hardened. 'What about the last couple of nights, Parrot? You were hanging around that waste ground at Leyland Street, weren't you?'

'No, not me!' Savoy backed away again and bumped against the table, a sudden stark, animal fear behind the words. 'I didn't go out. I wasn't as much as over the doorstep.'

'Then you won't mind us looking around.' Thane rose, watching him tremble. 'If you're fussy about things like a search-warrant, we'll stay here and get one sent round. But we're going to look, Parrot. Then you're coming back with us, for a longer talk.'

A bubbling moan came from Savoy, then he spun, one hand scrabbling at the table, and turned again, the long, saw-toothed bread-knife in his grip slashing a vicious arc.

Thane felt the knife rip at the cloth of his jacket and a rake of pain across his right shoulder. Conscious of Beech and Moss jumping forward, he grabbed the man's wrist as the blade pumped up again – then Savoy's free hand chopped down on his arm with numbing force and he had to let go.

97

'No.' Savoy's voice rose from a squawk to a screech and the round, spectacled face contorted in a blend of anger and terror. The knife fanned busily, keeping them back. 'I won't – nobody's locking me up again.'

'Easy now, Parrot.' Thane forced a calming note into the words. His shoulder still stung and his shirt was wet and sticky with blood. 'Nobody said anything about that.'

'No, you're clever.' The thick, powerful body tensed as Beech slightly shifted position. 'But I'm clever too – I know.'

Moss gave a gargantuan belch. For an instant, Savoy's attention switched at the sound – and Beech promptly heaved the table at him, dishes and cutlery flying as it knocked the man sideways.

Then they were on him, Thane grabbing again for the knife-wrist, Moss with an arm-lock round his throat, Beech diving in to take him at the knees and bring him down. But he still struggled wildly on the floor until the knife had been twisted out of his hand and his wrists had been handcuffed behind his back.

When that happened he stopped and lay sobbing with his body curled up in a tight, defensive ball.

'He'll need these. You keep them for now.' Moss scooped up Savoy's fallen spectacles from the floor and gave them to Beech. Then, for the first time, he saw the red stain spreading through the cloth of Thane's jacket. 'Damn that knife – let's see what it did.'

Thane let him help in easing the jacket off, then unbuttoned his shirt on his own. The knife had sliced a shallow three-inch gash high on his shoulder and the wound was still oozing blood. Padding a hand-kerchief over the gash, he waited while Beech tore a narrow strip from the grubby tablecloth. They tied the pad in place, then he fastened his shirt and eased his jacket on again.

Parrot Savoy remained curled on the floor, continuing to sob and hiding his face. Moss beckoned to Beech and together they heaved him off the floor and dumped him in one of the armchairs.

'The poor, stupid basket,' said Beech with a strained note of wonderment as Savoy tried to hide his face again. 'He – well, he didn't look that way, did he?'

'How are they supposed to look?' asked Thane wearily. His shoulder still hurt and he wished Savoy would stop that muffled, frightened wailing. 'Stay with him – and don't let him move. Phil, let's get on with it.'

Three other internal doors led off the apartment's hallway. The first was into a small bathroom and the second disclosed a slightly larger kitchen, where they gave the cupboards a cursory glance. Then Moss led the way to the remaining door. He opened it, met darkness, found the light switch, clicked it on, and gave a startled grunt. Looking over his shoulder, Thane's lips shaped a silent whistle of surprise.

Between them, they'd seen most things before – but seldom anything to compare with Parrot Savoy's private sanctuary. A secret sanctuary in an old red sandstone tenement block where craggy Scottish respectability could tolerate getting drunk on Saturday as long as it was followed by church on Sunday.

Swathes of purple velvet draped the walls and obscured the window. They met a thick, white wall-to-wall carpet – and everywhere were pictures of girls. Girls from calendar studies, girls cut from magazines, poster girls, they climbed the purple velvet and almost obscured the ceiling. They circled a mirror, they even met around the room's single lampshade.

A single ex-army sleeping-bag lay carefully rolled in the middle of the carpet, beside a cassette tape-player. The only item of furniture was a long wardrobe with sliding doors – doors covered in more girls.

Yet there was no menace in the room's atmosphere. It was more of an adolescent air, as if a sexually immature schoolboy had somehow managed to create a fantasy zone all of his own. Even the pin-ups reflected that mood.

'Do-it-yourself dreamland,' declared Moss and twisted a thin grin in Thane's direction. 'Whistle up one of our tame psychiatrists and he'd love this layout.'

Thane nodded. But the pain in his shoulder was another kind of reminder. Opening the first door of the wardrobe, he looked at the neatly hung clothes then reached in and drew out a heavy black sweater and black slacks. Both were stained with earth and had flecks of vegetation clinging to their folds.

'Colin –' Moss had opened the other door, and the wisping humour had gone from his manner.

Tossing the sweater and slacks beside the sleeping-bag, Thane joined him and understood. They'd found Parrot Savoy's trophy collection.

A woman's coat and a couple of dresses hung from the centre rail. Below them the open drawer spaces held a varied jumble of pants and bras, tights and stockings, even an old-fashioned suspender belt and the top half of a Baby Doll pyjama set.

'So he's a wash-day bandit too.' Moss probed the nearest pile with a cautious finger, as if something might jump out of the nylon and lace and bite. 'Minor league clothes-line grab and run stuff.'

It didn't match up to murder. Except that who could be sure what did and what didn't match up when it came to a crippled mind? Thane opened the wardrobe door wider then stopped over a row of shoes. Shoes with stiletto heels, shoes with platform soles, summer shoes, winter shoes – sometimes single, sometimes in pairs.

Among them was a pair of blue leather casuals with bright metal buckles.

He let Moss take the casuals and they went back to the other room. As they entered, Beech looked bewildered and stepped back from the chair where Savoy still crouched. The man had stopped sobbing and watched them anxiously, short-sighted eyes wide without their spectacles.

'Any trouble?' asked Thane.

Beech shook his head.

'Right.' Moss faced Savoy and showed him the blue shoes. His voice became surprisingly gentle. 'Where did you get these, Parrot?'

Giving a quick headshake, Savoy looked away.

'Come on, Harry.' Moss switched to the man's first name and showed a patience which would have surprised most of the everyday neds who crossed his path. 'You cleaned her windows, didn't you?'

'Yes.' It came like a whisper.

'But you didn't get the shoes at her house,' said Moss softly. 'We know that. You got them at Leyland Street, didn't you?'

Trying to hide his face against his shoulder, Savoy mumbled in a low, incoherent voice.

'It'll be all right, Harry,' tried Moss again with a glance at Thane. 'You see, it won't be prison this time. It – well, it'll be a sort of hospital where doctors understand about people like you. A hospital, Harry.' He nodded encouragingly as the man looked up. 'But the shoes first, Harry. We've got to know about them.'

'She was dead, so I didn't really do anything wrong,' said Parrot Savoy tearfully. 'She – I jus' took the shoes.' His broad shoulders twitched and the handcuffs jingled behind him. 'But you all think I killed her, right?'

'You mean you didn't?' asked Moss almost conversationally.

101

'No, mister.'

'Well then, what happened?'

'I'm not tellin' you,' said Parrot Savoy almost petulantly. 'Not unless you all promise to go away an' don't come back.'

'Harry –' Moss saw the waiting, animal-like determination on the man's face, stopped with a sigh.

Thane knew it was his turn.

'Beech,' he ordered quietly. 'Go and tell Erickson to radio for another car. Bring him back with you.'

Beech nodded and left. As the outside door clicked shut, Thane went over to Savoy, eased him forward in the chair, and removed the handcuffs.

'We'll do it your way, Parrot,' he agreed mildly. 'We'll go away – once you tell us what happened.'

'I tol' you I was clever, eh?' Savoy rubbed his wrists happily. 'All right, I'll tell you, mister. One thing I do is always keep a promise.'

He didn't see the glance that passed between the two detectives. But Moss took a moment before he spoke.

'What happened, Harry?'

'Well, it was two nights ago at the waste ground an' there was this man an' he was sort of dragging and carrying her in from the road –'

'About what time?'

'I never worry about time, mister.' Savoy shook his head. 'When I saw him I was frightened, but I hid an' watched. That's how I saw her shoes fall – he'd put them in her anorak pocket an' he was too busy carrying her to notice. So while he was busy putting her in that old car I nipped out to where they'd dropped. An' – an' then I ran away.'

'This man,' said Thane, praying they could keep the link to the twisted mind in that bulky body. 'What was he like?'

'A young bloke, I think. Thin too' – Savoy's brow furrowed – 'at least, I think so. It was dark, mister.'

'Did he have a car?'

Savoy shrugged. 'Don't know. I – I tol' you, I just got her nice shoes an' ran away.' He frowned. 'He shouldn't have done that to her. Still, I couldn't tell anyone because I knew they'd say I killed her.' Tears glistened in his eyes. 'Even though I don't hurt people.'

Thane thought of the bread-knife, but he didn't answer.

'You said she was dead, Harry,' said Moss softly. 'And you said you knew who she was – that means you went back, doesn't it?'

Savoy nodded unhappily. 'Just to look.'

'You didn't – well, touch her?'

'Me?' Indignation showed in the round face. 'I wouldn't do that. I – what would I do that for?' Then the indignation faded and he almost smiled at the shoes in Moss's hand. 'They're nice, aren't they?'

The outer door opened again and Beech came in with Erickson at his heels. Seeing them alarmed Savoy.

'You promised you'd go away,' he said with a quick agitation. 'You promised – an' now there's more of you ...'

'Sir.' Beech hesitated uneasily, taking in the scene. 'The other car is here – Control switched it from local patrol.'

'Good.' Thane gestured wearily towards Parrot Savoy. 'He's yours, Beech. Take him in, make it a holding charge of assault, then get a medical examiner over. But use the other car – we'll need Erickson and the duty car.'

Then he watched, tight-lipped, while Erickson and Beech between them took the whimpering, pathetically struggling figure towards the door.

'Nasty,' said Moss softly once they'd gone. 'Nasty but necessary. All right, what now?'

'Give me a choice and I'd settle for a good, stiff drink,' said Thane. He shook his head and glanced at his watch. 'The Glenrath office will be shut for the night by now, Phil. So – well, we'll go out and see the MacRath brothers on their home ground.'

'Plus mother?' Moss gave a cynical sniff. 'She should be interesting.'

Thane nodded and took a last look around the room. Then, prepared to believe every word of Parrot Savoy's story, he beckoned Moss towards the door.

Helensburgh and Glenrath House was a straight-line twenty-two mile drive west from Glasgow, mostly following the River Clyde as it widened into a shipping estuary. But the Millside car didn't go straight-line. First, it headed for the local general hospital where the casualty department showed no surprise at having to patch up still another cop.

Fifteen minutes later Colin Thane left with the gash on his shoulder covered by a dressing and adhesive tape. He'd borrowed a clean shirt from a mildly amused casualty surgeon and a nurse had sponged the worst of the staining from his jacket.

In that time he had changed his mind again. He had Erickson drive north-west, out of the city and through the low, green hills towards Drymen, where Doreen Ashton had gone to help her car club friends.

It was an eighteen-mile journey. From there back to Helensburgh, a commuter and resort town, would be another nineteen-mile distance. But it was a minor detour in terms of time, one Thane felt was overdue – and one that would also give him a chance to think.

For once, Phil Moss didn't grumble and sat silent, chewing an occasional stomach tablet and keeping his thoughts to himself. But for both of them what had happened with Parrot Savoy wasn't easy to forget.

The sun was beaming down through broken white cloud when Drymen village appeared ahead. They drove straight past its little white houses and forked off on a minor road which led into the Forestry Commission plantations and soon conditions changed radically. Tall, close-ranked firs pressed in on either side and became massed, dark greenery which had its roots in black, almost impenetrable shadow.

The road became a track. The Millside car bounced over a rough timber bridge which spanned a foaming torrent of water and a plump cock pheasant escaped their wheels by inches. A hare scurried frantically ahead then disappeared among the trees.

They were at the start of the Forest Two Hundred Rally's route and it was well signposted – beginning in a small clearing, an initial mile or so of twisting track had been carefully pennanted by the car club work party. Here and there a worse than average sump-shattering pothole had been filled in, but the rest had been left as motoring in the raw.

There was little else to see. The only vehicle that passed was a Land-Rover taking a load of bronzed forestry workers home at the end of their shift. The rest was the trees, the background rush of water and the occasional rustle of small, unseen animal life.

'You could lose a flaming army in there,' said Moss conversationally, scowling at the trees. 'Imagine trying to search through that lot.'

Thane nodded. The forest would have been an ideal killing ground, a nightmare for any investigation. At least they'd been spared that problem. He signalled to Erickson, the car turned on the brink of a deep drainage ditch, and they started towards their real destination.

That meant joining the Loch Lomond road, snaking along the tourist-clogged lochside, then branching off to climb through the hills past Glen Fruin – the old Glen of Sorrow, named for a forgotten clan battle hundreds of years before when bagpipes and the claymore had ruled much of Scotland.

The downhill stage towards Helensburgh had the Clyde as a broad, glinting background to the town. A black-hulled Polaris submarine back from patrol was nosing past some sailboats as it headed for the Gareloch nuclear base.

It was the kind of contrast which brought a wry twist to Thane's lips. Then he forgot about it as they neared Glenrath House.

About a mile before the town, the MacRath brothers' home had a driveway with rhododendron bushes in colour-splashed bloom and a view towards the water. In estate agent parlance it was a country house, Georgian in style, a little too small to be a mansion but still impressive. There was even a sign which said Tradesmen's Entrance pointing towards the rear and Moss chuckled derisively as they swept past it, to stop near the front door with gravel crunching under their tyres.

They left Erickson to read another of his law-books and went up to the front door. A heavy bell-push signalled somewhere deep in the house and after a minute the door swung open. A plump, middle-aged woman in a neat blue housekeeper's overall greeted them with a mild curiosity.

'Police.' Thane made the usual introductory noises. 'I'd like to talk to Mr Duncan MacRath – or his brother.'

The woman's smile faded at the edges but she invited them in, asked them to wait in the broad, oak-panelled hallway, and went off along a corridor.

'Gone to tell him there are nasty peasantry at the door,' muttered Moss acidly, looking around. 'It's always nice to see how the well-heeled live.'

'Once you know their credit rating,' said Thane good-humouredly. His eyes had strayed from a richly carved antique chest to a full-length portrait in oils which hung near a stairway. It showed a middle-aged man in country tweeds with the inevitable sheepdog at his feet. 'That's probably father MacRath.'

A small brass plate screwed to the bottom of the frame showed he was right and ended any doubts about where Duncan and Peter MacRath inherited their looks. The late John MacRath had been tall and slim, with the same strong, eagle-beaked face as his sons.

'Colin. Over here.'

The low-voiced urgency brought him round. Moss was frowning down at a telephone on a corner table, and when Thane joined him he pointed wordlessly at the exchange number on the dial.

It was 2161 – the number scribbled by Doreen Ashton on the crumpled slip of paper in Thane's wallet.

'Which of you is Chief Inspector Thane?' The crisp, unexpected voice behind them brought them round. A small, slim, elderly woman stood a few feet away, considering them with cool grey eyes. She had neat, blue-rinsed hair, wore a white sweater with tailored blue trousers, and had a thin gold necklace high at her throat. 'Jenny – our housekeeper – tells me you want to see my sons. I'm Victoria MacRath.'

She said her name like a challenge and Thane suddenly appreciated the warnings he'd been given. Victoria MacRath might be small and looked about sixty. But she had the air of a woman to whom command came easily and naturally and he remembered the Tradesmen's Entrance sign uneasily.

'Good evening, Mrs MacRath,' he said, smiling cheerfully. 'I'm Thane – and this is Detective Inspector Moss.'

'Thank you.' She gave a nod which conveyed she wasn't impressed, then ignored Moss. 'I'd like to know why you're here, Chief Inspector. Duncan and Peter have already given you statements about the Ashton girl – I don't see what more they can tell you.'

'Well, we hope they can maybe help again,' countered Thane easily. 'One or two fresh aspects have come up.'

'I see.' Victoria MacRath didn't hide her displeasure. 'Well, Duncan is here, working on his car. He's in the garage at the back of the house. But Peter has gone out – though if you wait, he should be back soon.'

'Maybe we could talk to you first, Mrs MacRath,' said Thane, and smiled as she raised a surprised eyebrow. 'You might be able to help too.'

Silently, she led the way through to a small sitting room which had a log fire smouldering in a stone hearth. An elderly sheepdog stirred briefly beside the fire, looked up at them, then lowered its head again.

'Well?' she asked once they were seated.

'You'll know Duncan gave Doreen Ashton a lift back to Glasgow the night she was murdered,' began Thane, choosing his words carefully. 'Then he told us he drove home –'

'And arrived soon after midnight,' she finished for him. Her voice chilled a fraction. 'Should I apologize for having been asleep by then?'

'No.' He twisted a grin. 'Peter was with you all evening?'

'Yes.' Her voice stayed chill. 'He brought home some work from the office and started it straight after dinner.'

And what about your housekeeper? Does she live in?'

'Yes, and I've already spoken to her – she did hear Duncan's car but she was in bed and paid no attention to the time.' Victoria MacRath paused and glanced at Moss. 'If your – ah – colleague wants to talk to her –'

'Please.' He nodded to Moss, who rose obediently and ambled out.

Victoria MacRath took a cigarette from a jar, struck a match to light it with a quick, impatient gesture, and drew on the smoke lightly.

'Now we're alone, it's my turn, Chief Inspector,' she said suddenly in a sharp, business-like voice. 'What the hell is this all about?' The lines of age on her face showed more clearly as she frowned. 'Are you seriously considering my stepson could be involved in this girl's death?'

'Your stepson?' Thane showed his surprise.

She sighed. 'Yes, if the label matters. My husband's first wife died when Duncan was about a year old. We married about a year later – there's exactly three years between Duncan and Peter. But for all practical purposes they're both mine. And I'm still waiting for an answer, Chief Inspector.'

'The answer is I don't know,' said Thane, caught off guard. 'Did you ever meet Doreen Ashton?'

'A few times.' Her free hand fingered the thin gold chain at her throat. 'In the office, though I don't go there so often now. She seemed good at her job, which was what mattered.'

'And when you heard she'd been murdered?'

'I was shocked, of course. But Duncan –' she shook her head incredulously – 'even the idea is ludicrous. All he thinks about is that damned rally car.'

'No steady girl friend?'

'No.' Her mouth twitched slightly. 'I can assure you he's perfectly normal and I could name a few girls I'm fairly certain could confirm it. But before you ask, he certainly wasn't interested in Doreen Ashton.'

'We know Doreen was worried about something,' said Thane quietly. 'When she was killed she was carrying a slip of paper with your telephone number on it, Mrs MacRath. I'd like to know why.'

'I'm sorry, I can't help.' She drew on the cigarette again with a frown. 'The girl certainly didn't telephone here. As far as I know, she never has at any time. You – ah – say she was worried?'

He nodded. 'There were two numbers, Mrs MacRath. The other was Millside police.'

'I still can't help.' Victoria MacRath gave a puzzled shake of her head. 'Perhaps she thought that if the police couldn't come to her aid she might turn to us.'

'Could it have been any kind of business worry, Mrs MacRath?'

'I doubt it.' The room seemed to chill several degrees in an instant. 'We are a family firm, Chief Inspector – and our firm is in a very healthy state.'

'I had to ask.'

'And you've been answered.' Her grey eyes were steely. 'Isn't there also a young policeman involved in your inquiries?'

'Who told you that?' he asked, surprised.

'Duncan – he mentioned it, anyway. Of course, that may be the kind of possibility you prefer to leave aside.' She rose deliberately. 'I'm glad we had our talk, Chief Inspector.'

Thane got to his feet, thanked her stonily, and was left to walk out of the room on his own. He reached the hallway at the same time as Moss came wandering back from the kitchen area.

'Forget the housekeeper,' said Moss gloomily. 'Queen Victoria was right – she heard a car, but doesn't know when. Oh, and she had a couple of hours off in the evening. But Victoria and Peter were

110

here when she left, and she said goodnight to Victoria when she got back. So – how did you get on?'

'Badly.' Thane left it at that. 'Let's find Duncan.'

They went out, drew a grin from Erickson as they passed the Millside car, and walked round to the rear of the house. The garage was at the back of a large courtyard, big enough to hold three cars in comfort, but the only vehicle in sight was the black rally Ford Capri. The front end was jacked up, and Duncan MacRath was working around the nearside brakes.

He heard their feet on the stone floor, looked up, and showed surprise. Then, wiping his hands on the front of his overalls, he came up to meet them.

'More questions?' he asked suspiciously.

'A couple,' agreed Thane neutrally. He went past MacRath towards the car and ran a hand along the roofline. 'Problems?'

'None I can't cope with.' MacRath remained suspicious and combed back his long dark hair with one grimy hand. 'Well, what is it this time?'

'Any idea why Doreen Ashton should be carrying your house telephone number around with her?' asked Thane bluntly.

MacRath blinked. 'No.'

'Not even a business reason?' queried Moss.

'No.' MacRath gave a groan of despair. 'Look, before you ask, she was our secretary, I was friendly with her, but end. I didn't bed down with her on the side.'

'Did she bed with Robby Deacon?' asked Thane bluntly.

'Muck-raking time, is it?' MacRath turned away from them, went over to the garage work-bench, and picked up a heavy spanner. 'Go away, Chief Inspector. I'm busy – two days from now I'm in a rally I damned well want to win. If it helps satisfy you, I've seen her clown around with Deacon. Clown – nothing more.'

The sound of a car approaching brought a look of relief to his face. A grey Jaguar coupé purred into the courtyard, stopped and Peter MacRath climbed out.

Looking as unfriendly as Duncan, he came over and stood beside him.

'I know we gave an invitation,' said Peter sharply. 'But I didn't expect to see you two so quickly.'

'Everybody seems in a welcoming mood today,' said Thane dryly. 'We had a problem. Duncan can tell you about it.'

The fair-haired man glanced at Duncan MacRath, who nodded.

'It can keep, Peter. It was simple enough.'

'Well – all right. Forget the acid, Chief Inspector,' said Peter MacRath with a degree of reluctance. 'But we've had a bad day.' He brightened and turned to his stepbrother again. 'I saw the girls, Duncan. It's fixed – I said we'd collect them at nine.'

Duncan MacRath pursed his lips and glanced at the rally car. 'I don't know. I've a lot to do here.'

'Nothing that can't wait, man.' Peter MacRath turned to Thane for support. 'I've a couple of girls lined up and an invite to a party in town. What would you do?'

'Ask my wife first,' said Thane sadly.

They left the brothers and went back to the Millside car. Erickson swung round from the driving wheel as they climbed aboard.

'Where now, sir?'

'Home to Millside,' answered Thane. 'Erickson, how would you like to clock up some overtime tonight?'

'I could use the money,' agreed Erickson easily. 'What's the job?'

'Robby Deacon – you find him, you talk to him. You're a friendly cop who wears the same uniform and you've a common interest in cars. Off-duty, you

112

think all C.I.D. are hard bastards and it isn't your fault you have to drive me around.' Thane saw Erickson's widening grin and quelled it quickly. 'Don't overdo things. But I want him to feel you're a shoulder he can weep on.'

Erickson nodded and began humming to himself as he started the car.

'And what about them?' demanded Moss, thumbing towards the house.

'Victoria MacRath wouldn't weep on anybody's shoulder,' said Thane wryly. 'More likely she'd bite. We'll have to tackle them another way. But tomorrow, Phil – not tonight.'

Tonight he was going home. There was always a time when it paid to wait a little, to let events shape their own future before he moved in.

Chapter Five

Millside Police Station seemed quiet when the duty car stopped outside. But it was usually that way around nine p.m. – the day-time incidents had been tidied and another hour or so would pass before the night-time drunks and petty assaults began flowing in.

The only unwelcome sight was the Headquarters car parked at the main door. Inside the building, the duty sergeant at the public counter caught Thane's eye and gave a warning grimace towards the C.I.D. stairway. At the top of the stairs, the main C.I.D. room had the usual number of night team men in occupancy but instead of the normal gossiping atmosphere every single one seemed to have found some task to keep him busy – and the door of Thane's private office lay wide open.

'Do you need me along?' asked Moss with a distinct lack of enthusiasm. 'I could go and hide in a cupboard or something.'

'I need your unquestioning loyal support,' Thane told him dryly. 'Come on.'

They went in together. The bulky figure of Buddha Ilford occupied Thane's chair. Wearing off-duty sweater and slacks, the city C.I.D. chief was scowling at the sports pages of an evening paper and folded it slowly before he greeted them with a curt nod.

114

'I'm told you've been busy,' he said bleakly. 'In fact, a certain female damned nearly chewed my ear off over the phone about you, Thane.'

'Victoria MacRath?' Thane nodded with no particular surprise. 'We didn't exactly get on the same wavelength, sir.'

'I'd reckon that the understatement of the year,' snarled Ilford. He dragged his battered, blackened pipe from the top pocket of his sweater and used the stem like a pointer. 'Instead of staying at home with my feet up, I only got rid of her by promising I'd come here and find out what the hell you've been playing at. So – tell me.'

Thane glanced at Moss, but that individual merely gave a fractional shrug of his thin shoulders and eased towards the window, out of Ilford's direct line of fire.

'I asked her a few questions,' admitted Thane.

'One inferring the family firm might be on the rocks,' said Ilford grimly. 'I'd call that a splendid example of your well-known tact.'

'She wasn't meant to like it,' said Thane. He stuck his hands in his pockets and met Ilford's glare with a wooden determination. 'Of course, I didn't have a full list of Glenrath's clients in front of me.'

Ilford reddened. 'All right, just for the record, I'm on that list. I had an insurance policy mature a couple of years back and – well, damn you, the rest doesn't matter. You knew anyway, didn't you?'

'It was more or less spelled out, sir. By Peter MacRath.'

'I was advised by a certain judge that whisky was a good investment.' Ilford squirmed a little in the chair. 'Well, it's still incidental. We're talking about murder – I've heard fragments of all that's been happening but let's hear your version.'

Thane told him while Ilford grimly filled and lit the pipe and smoked in silence. The C.I.D. chief gave a long sigh at the finish.

'Well, the shoes you found at Parrot Savoy's place have been identified by the girl's friends,' he contributed wearily. 'Take it his story is true – and it sounds like it could be. The medical examiners agree he's mentally unsound and we'll have to go for a committal to a state hospital. Which in turn means you can't use him as any kind of a witness.'

'Amen,' said Moss softly from the window.

Ilford nodded a grudging agreement. 'Any other outside prospects on the horizon, Thane?'

'No, sir.'

'Remove Duncan MacRath and you're left with young Robby Deacon.' Ilford grimaced at the prospect. 'I spoke to Superintendent Chadwick at the Training Centre. He reckons Deacon is one of the brightest rookie prospects we've had for a long time.'

'He may be bright, but right now he's behaving like an idiot,' said Thane bitterly. 'If I could only get something positive out of the post-mortem examination –'

'Why strangle a dead girl?' Ilford grunted and glanced at his watch. 'Well, it was a good try at a cover-up, and it's only thanks to Doc Williams it didn't come off.' He got to his feet. 'I'm leaving. There's a TV show I don't want to miss. But for God's sake tread warily with Victoria MacRath if you can.'

'I'll try, sir,' promised Thane neutrally.

'That's all I ask,' sighed Ilford. 'Frankly, she terrifies me.' He reached the door, opened it, and then looked back. 'Incidentally, the four Spaniards you've got locked up may get off the hook.'

'Sir?'

'The Spanish consul has been making pleading noises, their ship genuinely can't sail without them, and the result is a general howl of alarm,' explained

116

Ilford. 'The suggestion is that as nobody else was involved or hurt we settle for a lower charge of disorderly conduct all round – and some fairly hefty fines.'

'*Viva España*,' said Moss caustically. 'If they'd been four of our locals –'

'They're not,' countered Ilford and gave a wisp of a grin. 'Anyway I like Spaniards – I always to go Spain on holiday.'

He went out, the door closed, and Moss gave a despairing gesture.

'Can we do anything right?' he demanded.

'Forget it.' Thane checked the papers on his desk and stacked them in an untidy heap for the morning. 'Come on – this once I'll let Mary feed you.'

Mary Thane was used to their kind of invasion, even though she was midway through getting Tommy and Kate packed off to bed.

That came to a halt when they arrived, with Moss the centre of attraction and the dog barking excitedly for good measure. But eventually both children were shoved upstairs under various threats, Clyde gave up trying to lick Moss's face, and by then Mary had a meal waiting on the table.

She let them eat in silence then, as they sat back over a final cup of coffee, she looked at Thane quizzically.

'Is this a passing-through visit or do I have a husband for tonight?'

'Good question,' said Moss, burping gently. 'Mary, if you were married to an older, more considerate character like me –'

'Then she'd really have something to worry about,' said Thane sardonically. He twisted a grin at his wife, some distinctly carnal thoughts stirring. 'I'm staying.'

'It helps to know,' she mused, then, more seriously, went on: 'It's a rough one, isn't it, Colin?'

He nodded, not asking how much she'd heard. Police wives had a grapevine all of their own, with roots that reached into surprising places.

'Rough on people, anyway.' He thought of young Deacon and shrugged. 'It could get rougher. What we really need is some kind of lead on what the Ashton girl was getting so uptight about. But we couldn't get it at her apartment, there was nothing apparent at her office –'

'And that includes her desk,' added Moss. Tail wagging lazily, Clyde had settled at his feet. He reached down and scratched the dog behind one ear. 'She was a tidy girl – nothing left lying around.'

'I know the kind. Colin thought he'd married one.' Mary Thane glanced round the room, scattered with the day's debris, and grimaced. 'If she'd seen this lot she'd file it under P for Problems.'

'Maybe.' Thane grinned a little and reached for his cigarettes. 'Phil, she'd have a shorthand notebook –'

'Full of shorthand, end. I looked.'

'But if we knew what she'd been doing there a week ago, when she first began making noises –' Thane stopped there as the telephone rang.

Mary answered it, but the call was for Thane. He took the receiver from her with a grimace, then heard John Kelso's voice at the other end. The Customs and Excise man sounded oddly subdued.

'Colin, I think we should have a meeting tomorrow,' he said without preamble. 'About eleven – could you make it?'

'Yes.' Thane sensed a slight embarrassment behind the words. 'Heard anything?'

'In a way. I – I'd rather leave it till tomorrow.' Kelso's manner didn't brook argument. 'At the new bonded warehouse in Liberty Street, all right?'

'I'll be there,' promised Thane, and hung up.

When he went back, Phil Moss was getting ready to leave for his boarding-house room. He told him about Kelso's message, they talked for a couple of minutes longer about the next day's programme, then Moss left.

Mary was through in the kitchen, tidying things away. He came up quietly behind her, put his arms round her waist, then kissed her when she turned.

A little later, they decided the dishes could wait till morning. He also had to explain about his shoulder, but that was later too.

Friday came up cloudily with a hint of rain in the air. But Friday was always a cheerful day around the city – mainly because it was pay-day – and the morning rush-hour traffic lacked some of its usual antagonism as Thane drove from his home to Millside Division.

He, got there about eight-thirty, left his Hillman station wagon in the fenced-in parking lot and got out at the same time as the Olympic Flame emerged from a battered Volkswagen.

'Heard the latest about your damned Spaniards?' demanded Chief Inspector Greystone abruptly. He'd cut himself shaving and had a blood-smear on his shirt collar. 'Now we're letting them go with a fine! They've been a complete, farcical waste of time.'

'They're not my Spaniards,' said Thane thankfully. 'Right now they're yours. But next time I'll remember and let them kill each other.'

The sarcasm was wasted and he parted thankfully from Greystone at the C.I.D. stairway. Going up he checked the occurrence book, for new overnight entries, then went through to where Sergeant MacLeod had a kettle boiling peacefully in the duty room. MacLeod had a tall figure in civilian clothes with him, but it wasn't till the man turned that Thane recognized Erickson out of uniform.

'I've got the morning off to attend a law class, sir,' explained the Millside driver cheerfully. 'I'm just looking in to report about last night.'

'And log your overtime in the book,' suggested Thane dryly. He led the way into his room then asked, 'Did you find Deacon?'

'No problems,' grinned Erickson. 'He was at the Newfield service station, working on his car. I used my own car, drove in like an ordinary customer, gave him the big hello, and it was easy after that.' Erickson paused and rubbed his left ear thoughtfully. 'He's – well, a pretty likeable character.'

'Did I ask for a character assessment?' queried Thane.

'No, sir.' Erickson didn't let it worry him. 'There was a girl with him, a redhead. He called her Kate.'

'Katherine Manson.' Thane remembered her in Deacon's intake at the Training Centre. 'How would you rate them – just good friends?'

'A girl like her?' Erickson chuckled and shook his head. 'That would be a hell of a waste. No, I'd say they were pretty close.'

'And Deacon?'

'Worried.' Erickson became thoughtful again. 'Edgy with it, like he wasn't sure what to do next. Uh – one thing, sir. He's out of this Forest Two Hundred Rally – his car has a broken piston and he hasn't a hope in hell of getting it fixed in time.'

'What did he say about Doreen Ashton?'

'Not much. Just that when he looked in that car and saw her he wished he'd never thought of being a cop.'

There was nothing more. Erickson left, Sergeant MacLeod wandered in with the day's first mug of coffee and some report forms, and Thane sat for a moment sipping the coffee and ignoring the paper.

Then he reached for the telephone, called the Training Centre and located Sergeant Easter.

'When is Robby Deacon due with you next?' he demanded.

'He's here now, sir,' croaked the Easter Bunny over the line. 'We've a special lecture session this mornin' – want me to get hold of him for you?'

'No,' said Thane quickly. 'I'm coming out – but don't tell him.'

He hung up, finished his coffee at a gulp, and went through to Sergeant MacLeod's desk.

'Mac, when Phil Moss arrives tell him I've gone to the Training Centre. I want him to meet me at the Glenrath Investment office in an hour.'

Nodding, MacLeod scribbled a note on his pad. Then he looked up, mildly curious.

'What's happening at the Centre, sir?'

'If I'm right, a plain, old-fashioned gutting,' said Thane grimly. 'You'll hear about it, Mac. Don't worry.'

At the Police Training Centre, he left his car in the courtyard parking area beside a Land-Rover which had Army Bomb Disposal markings on its doors. The Centre itself seemed oddly quiet, then he noticed the way most of the windows in the courtyard had been opened and understood.

Walking through the courtyard he homed on a growing hum of voices coming from the rear of the Centre. About fifty rookie cops were there, standing in a semi-circle on a patch of waste ground where an old slum tenement had been pulled down. They had their backs to him and were facing a khaki-clad army sergeant, who was flanked by several of the Training Centre instructors.

Quietly, Thane eased closer. He'd seen bomb-disposal demonstrations before, he was more intent on spotting Deacon, but the army sergeant's quiet, matter-of-fact explanations still caught his attention.

'Like I've told you, any fool can make a bomb,' said the sergeant cheerfully. He was young, but he had the ribbon of the Distinguished Service Medal on his battledress tunic and that wasn't handed out for passing aptitude tests. 'You can buy everything you need in any hardware store. Should you find a bomb, don't muck about with it. You get everybody clear and send for some idiot like me to do the necessary.'

There were grins and some muttered comments from the probationers. Thane saw Robby Deacon over to the left of the semi-circle, near the front, and began to edge nearer.

'However, you might find something that looks quite harmless. Something like this.' The sergeant stopped, opened a box at his feet, and drew out a tiny aluminium cylinder no bigger than a cigarette's filter tip. 'This is a blasting detonator. It looks like a toy – but it sets off a main charge. Let's see what it can do on its own.'

An elbow nudged Thane's side and he found Sergeant Easter standing beside him.

'I can get Deacon now, sir,' said the Easter Bunny in a hoarse whisper.

'When this finishes,' Thane told him quietly. 'Get the Manson girl too. Tell them I want to see them back in the courtyard.'

Easter raised a surprised eyebrow but left while Thane watched the rest of the demonstration. The army sergeant had taken another detonator from his box, one with a thin electrical flex running from it. Solemnly, one of the instructors came forward carrying a king-sized raw beefsteak on a plate. The sergeant took the beefsteak, wrapped it round the tiny capsule, and laid the meat on the ground.

122

'Now imagine that beefsteak is your hand,' he said grimly. 'You've picked up a detonator. You're just holding it.'

The instructors stepped back. There was a sudden, sharp bang, the beefsteak jumped several feet in the air, and the nearest of the recruits were spattered with bloodied fragments.

'That could be your hand,' said the sergeant quietly. 'Detonators are fragile things – sometimes body heat can be enough to set them off.' He looked round to make sure the lesson had got home, then grinned. 'Well, that's your Commandant's lunch gone up in bits. Now I'm going to set up a bigger bang, a coffee-pot bomb. It'll take a couple of minutes, so take a break for a smoke if you like.'

The senior instructor nodded, the recruits began to drift into groups, and Thane turned and went back to the empty courtyard.

Standing beside his car, he lit a cigarette and waited. A minute passed, then Robby Deacon and Katherine Manson appeared. They saw him, hesitated, Deacon muttered to the red-haired girl, and then they came over.

'Sergeant Easter said you wanted to see me – both of us, I mean, Chief Inspector,' said Deacon awkwardly.

'I do.'

Silently, Thane considered them for a moment and the girl flushed under his gaze. A tiny fleck of beefsteak from the demonstration had landed on the shoulder of her tunic and she seemed unaware of it. Reaching out, he flicked it away, then ignored her and switched his attention to Deacon.

Deacon swallowed. 'Sir, I –'

'When I want you to speak, I'll tell you,' said Thane harshly.

'Sir.' The lanky youngster jerked as if stung and stiffened.

'Now.' Thane tossed his cigarette away and drew a deep breath. 'Deacon, you're supposed to be bright, even intelligent. Some people still have the notion you might make a good cop – but right now I'm not one of them. I wouldn't give you a job as a tea-boy.'

The girl made a faint protesting noise and he switched in her direction.

'And you – right now remember you're not Kate Manson as far as I'm concerned. You're a probationer policewoman and another damned fool if you know even half of what's been going on.'

She bit her lip and the flush deepened.

'I'm dealing with a murder case,' said Thane in a voice like crushed ice. 'A girl about your age, Policewoman Manson. She had good looks, like you. She enjoyed living – like you. You can see her if you want, in the City Mortuary. Or you can ask Deacon what she looked like when he found her.'

'He – he told me,' she said in a low voice.

'Did he?' Thane glanced briefly at Deacon then came back to her. 'Did he also tell you things have reached the stage where I could build a damned good set of reasons for having him as a suspect?'

He didn't let them answer but brought out his wallet and produced the photograph he'd found in Doreen Ashton's room.

'What about this?' He held the photograph grimly under the younger man's nose. 'You look pretty cosy with her in it. Would you still say Doreen Ashton was just "someone you knew"?'

Deacon stared at the photograph and moistened his lips. 'I – I'd forgotten it was taken,' he blurted. 'We were fooling around at a car club evening, that's all. I told you the truth.'

'Like you always do?' asked Thane derisively.

124

'Did you mean what you said, Chief Inspector?' asked Katherine Manson suddenly, her voice husky and earnest. 'Do people seriously think Robby might have killed her?'

Thane nodded. 'It's a possibility. One of them anyway.'

'I know he didn't,' said the girl quietly.

'Because you were with him?'

'Yes.' She gave a wry smile in Deacon's direction. 'That's why he left those car club people early. And the following night – the night he found her body – we were going to meet again.'

'Can you prove any of that?'

She nodded reluctantly. 'The first night, if necessary. But it would mean involving a girl friend.'

'Kate's right, sir,' said Deacon unhappily. 'What I told you before was – well, I was just trying to keep Kate out of it.'

'Being gallant about it?' Thane regarded him stonily then glanced at Katherine Manson, his mouth tightening. Inwardly, his anger was mixed with something close to relief. 'If you two want to have a tumble somewhere it doesn't matter a damn to me.'

'As long as we're out of uniform and the handcuffs don't jingle?' The red-haired girl forced a short, wry laugh. 'It isn't so simple, Chief Inspector. You don't know my family – I've a father who would go berserk. And can you imagine what it would be like for us here, on the training course, if it got out?'

'Whose idea was it to stay quiet?' asked Thane wearily.

'Mine, sir.' Deacon shuffled his feet. 'But you gave me the idea.'

'Eh?' Thane stared at him.

Deacon nodded solemnly. 'Your lecture, sir. You said a cop should know how to exercise discretion. I thought that was all I was doing.'

Thane closed his eyes and swore long, savagely and out loud. Then, with a sigh, he considered them again.

'Go away,' he said bitterly. 'Go away, both of you.'

Deacon moistened his lips. 'You'll probably have to report this, sir. We know that. But – well, what will happen?'

Thane restrained himself with an effort.

'You said discretion,' he reminded savagely. 'If you're lucky, you'll maybe still end up pounding a beat together – in Outer Mongolia.'

They looked at each other, bewildered. Then Deacon snapped a quick salute and they went off. But, after a few paces, Katherine Manson stopped and came back.

'Sir –'

'Well?' asked Thane wearily.

'We'll invite you to the wedding.' She hesitated, then quickly kissed him on the cheek. 'Thanks.'

Before Thane had really recovered she was off again. They vanished from the courtyard – and a second later a loud explosion came from the waste ground. Every window in the Training Centre rattled.

Thane sighed, got into his car and started it up.

Phil Moss was waiting more or less patiently outside the Glenrath office when he arrived. Millside C.I.D.'s second-in-command was wearing a clean shirt, a minor event, though the shirt seemed to have lost most of its buttons.

'If I'd been left here much longer I'd have taken root,' complained Moss. 'What was this gabble Mac gave me about the Training Centre?'

'I saw Robby Deacon again. We can forget him.' Thane sketched what had happened.

'Discretion, he called it?' Moss shaped a delighted

126

expression of near disbelief. 'Are you going to let him get away with that?'

'I'll make sure he has his backside kicked every time he does anything more than breathe from now on,' promised Thane bleakly. 'And you can watch me tear up those damned lecture notes. I've learned a lesson too.'

Moss managed to stop grinning by the time they reached the counter at the Glenrath outer office. The same pimple-faced young clerk came forward, recognized them, and reached for the internal telephone. Thane stopped him.

'What's your name, son?' he asked.

'Tony – Tony Dennis.' The youngster eyed him cautiously.

'Tony, last time I was here you told me Doreen Ashton was the friendly type and you liked her. Did you notice if she got many outside telephone calls?'

Dennis frowned. 'A few, Chief Inspector. I wouldn't say many.'

'From men?' Thane saw the youngster was puzzled. 'I mean lately – did she have more calls than usual or any that seemed to upset her?'

'No.' Dennis shook his head. 'I – think I'd have noticed.'

'I think you would,' agreed Thane softly.

A minute later he and Moss were shown into Duncan MacRath's private office. Peter MacRath was with the dark-haired rally driver, both of them seated at the glass-topped table in the middle of the room with coffee cups in front of them.

'Good morning,' said Duncan MacRath dryly. 'You two are getting to be part of our way of life.' He glanced at his stepbrother. 'We should find out if they're tax-deductible.'

'We could claim they were a business liability.' Peter MacRath grinned with a wary tolerance. Overnight, his left arm had acquired a dark-coloured sling and his wrist was heavily strapped. With his other hand he pushed out a chair for Thane. 'Sit down, both of you. What do you want this time?'

'It won't take long.' Thane settled in the chair while Moss dragged out another 'We need another look around Doreen Ashton's office.'

The two MacRaths exchanged an odd glance and Duncan gave a fractional shrug.

'Go ahead,' he said resignedly. 'But I thought you were finished there. What's happening, Chief Inspector? Have you any clear lead yet to who killed Doreen?'

'Let's say we're still eliminating possibilities.' Thane gestured towards Peter MacRath's sling. 'Been fighting a war somewhere?'

The fair-haired man glanced sheepishly at his step-brother. 'I fell down some stairs. We – well, that party Duncan and I went to last night got hectic.'

'Hectic is an understatement.' Duncan MacRath's rugged face twisted wryly. 'And it leaves me with a problem. This idiot was supposed to be my co-driver in the Forest Two Hundred – take care of the navigation side for me. But he can't do that with a damaged wrist, so I've got exactly till midnight to find a substitute.'

'Map-reading stuff?' Phil Moss grimaced at the notion. 'I wouldn't volunteer.'

'It's not so difficult.' Peter MacRath opened a folder in front of him and spread some broadly spaced typed sheets of paper on the table. 'We use these – pace notes.' He looked at the sheets a moment and shook his head sadly. 'This was one of the last typing jobs Doreen did for us.'

Thane picked up a sheet and tried to read the apparent gibberish of letters and numerals it contained. But he gave up.

128

'It's easier than it looks,' said Duncan. 'Before an event like this I can take a practice drive over the rally route. I make my own notes as I go along – every driver has his own ideas. I decide things like how fast to take a bend, where there's a reasonable straight ahead, problem spots I want to remember. If you've got a good navigator, he doesn't need to have seen the route at all. Give him your notes, a map and a stop-watch and he just sits beside you and reads it off.'

'I'll give you a translation,' volunteered Peter MacRath. He lifted the nearest sheet. 'This part. FR into ML 300 humps. MR into SL brow flat 700. Translation, Chief Inspector – fast right bend into a medium left, then a three hundred yard straight over humps. A medium right bend into a slow left – slow means you take it slow, or else. Then over the brow and go flat out. Simple.'

'I'll take your word for it,' said Thane neutrally. 'When does the rally start?'

'The first car leaves at one minute past midnight, then the rest follow at one minute intervals.' Duncan MacRath sucked his teeth and gave a determined grunt. 'I'll be one of them, even if I've got to put Victoria herself in the passenger seat.'

'I'd come to watch that happen.' Thane saw Moss glance at his watch, nodded, and rose. 'All right if we check the room now?'

'Yes, as long as you don't need us. We've some work to get through.' Duncan MacRath flicked a switch on the intercom box beside him. 'I'll get Tony Dennis to stay with you. He can help if you've any problems.'

The young clerk answered the summons and took them through to Doreen Ashton's office, a small room with a typing desk, a locker and a stationery cabinet.

'I went through the drawers last time,' reminded Moss, gesturing towards the desk. 'Same again?'

'Let's try it.' Thane looked round at Dennis. 'Tony, where would she keep her correspondence files, letter carbons – that kind of thing?'

'Not here.' Dennis shook his head. 'We keep a central file room for everything like that. She only kept – well, stationery and personal stuff in here.'

'Then who cleaned these out?' demanded Moss in a sudden, angry growl. He had some of the desk drawers open and stood scowling down at them. 'They've been damned well emptied – emptied down to the last paper clip!'

'Was that wrong?' Victoria MacRath's voice came unexpectedly from behind them. They turned and saw her standing in the open doorway, slight and deceptively fragile in a dark green two-piece outfit.

'I'm afraid I'm to blame, Chief Inspector,' she said almost contritely.

'You?' Thane took a deep breath. 'Mind telling me why?'

'I was told you'd already looked in here.' She came into the room and gave Tony Dennis a fractional nod of dismissal. The young clerk left quickly, glad to escape.

'We looked,' agreed Thane. 'That didn't mean we were finished.'

'Oh?' Victoria MacRath's grey eyes met his calmly, the little crow-foot lines of age around them crinkling with something that wasn't quite sympathy. 'I'm sorry, but I didn't know that. So I threw out anything that seemed trivial – I felt it better for the rest of the staff if reminders of that kind weren't lying about.'

'What happened to the stuff?' asked Moss aggressively.

'I packed everything into a cardboard box yesterday afternoon. The box went out with the office rubbish last night and would be collected first thing this morning.' Victoria MacRath pursed her thin lips. 'The few

130

things I thought should be kept for relatives who might want them are in another cardboard box. It's at the bottom of that locker.'

She watched silently while they brought out the box and cut the string around its lid. Inside was a small clock, an empty leather purse and a few other everyday items.

Slowly, Thane replaced the lid and faced the woman. Sunlight from the window glinted off her blue-rinsed hair like a smoke-coloured halo and for a moment he thought he saw an expression of vindictive triumph in her eyes. Then it had gone.

'We'll take these with us,' he said in a flat voice. 'That way you can really forget about her.'

Victoria MacRath flinched but said nothing and stood back to let them leave.

'She's a hard old bitch,' pronounced Phil Moss once they were outside the building. He nodded at the box under Thane's arm. 'We won't get anything out of that lot.'

'No. But I didn't want to leave them.' Thane looked speculatively at the office block. 'Mother Bear is getting worried about her cubs.'

'That's when Mother Bears get really dangerous, isn't it?' Moss scowled at an innocent pedestrian who was passing then grinned as the man quickly increased his pace. 'I'd like to go back in there with a search warrant, just for the hell of it.'

'I'd like to do it with a better reason.' The thought reminded Thane of his next move. 'Phil, I've got to get to that Customs bonded warehouse. I want you to find Doc Williams and tell him we must get some sense out of the post-mortem tests – the sooner the better.'

131

There was a taxi rank further down the street and Moss headed towards it. Thane climbed aboard his car, put the cardboard box on the seat beside him, and started the engine with the hope that John Kelso might have something tangible to offer him.

The bonded warehouse at Liberty Street was big, brand new, and built like a fort – which in a way it was, defending several million gallons of raw whisky till the time when the liquor would be ready for commercial use and a greedy government could reap its tax share from every gallon.

John Kelso had left word with the gate guards to expect Thane. But even so, he had to produce identification and wait under their scrutiny until Kelso appeared, signed him into a visitor book, and took him through a door which was locked behind them.

Thane looked around. They were in a vast warehouse area, filled with tiered rows of giant whisky casks. Each wooden cask, numbered, iron-hooped and bearing the name of its original distillery, held one hundred gallons. Just one tiered row of them had a value far beyond what most men could earn in a lifetime.

'We collected over three hundred million pounds in Excise Duty from whisky last year,' said John Kelso, as if guessing his thoughts. The Customs man sighed, his voice quiet in the cathedral-like atmosphere of the silent warehouse. 'I never drink the stuff myself – gin is my tipple. Maybe that's just as well, or every time I had a whisky I'd be thinking about how three-quarters of the cost is pure tax.'

'Unless you drink it abroad.' Automatically, Thane voiced the ritual complaint. Exported whisky was free of British tax, and a Scot abroad could usually sample his native beverage a lot more cheaply than at home.

'John, I didn't come to discuss the iniquities of life. You said you had something for me on the Glenrath outfit.'

'Yes.' Kelso patted the nearest cask affectionately. 'I thought – well, if you came here it might help you to understand. Whisky isn't like ordinary commerce, more a way of life, with a lot of trust.' He chewed his lip for a moment. 'I went through our records again, Colin. There's nothing, absolutely nothing there on which we could default the Glenrath operation. But if you want gossip, not fact –'

'The way things are going, I'll settle for anything,' said Thane frankly. 'Let's have it.'

'A story I heard when I was – well, asking around.' Kelso spoke uncomfortably. 'It seems there was quite a row recently about one of Glenrath's client holdings. The client died and the family swore blind that Glenrath was fiddling them out of a lot of money. Their lawyer thought so too – it was settled eventually, but he still goes around saying he wouldn't trust Glenrath further than he can spit.'

Thane gave a thin whistle of interest. 'What's his name?'

'Daniel Cockcroft.' Kelso frowned. 'Remember, I got this as third- or fourth-hand gossip. But –'

'But it still matters.' Thane had met Daniel Cockcroft around the courts. He was the quieter kind of Scottish solicitor, who made his money by results rather than by publicity. 'I'll try him.'

'Let me know if anything happens.' Kelso's mild, brown, button-like eyes showed a quick concern. 'If there is a problem, then my Department has its own interests to protect.'

'If I find they're syphoning off booze through an underground pipeline you'll be the first to know,' promised Thane with a grin.

Kelso had to escort him back through the security doors to the gatehouse exit. They said goodbye, with a final promise from Thane to keep in touch, and then the Customs man went back to his casks and calculations.

Thane drove in towards the city and Daniel Cockcroft's office. But when he got there the lawyer was out and his secretary said he was likely to be in court until late in the afternoon. Disappointed, but telling her that he would be back, Thane used one of the law office telephones to call Millside Division.

'Just checking in,' he said when Sergeant MacLeod's voice answered one of the C.I.D. extensions.

'I'm glad you did, sir,' MacLeod's voice rumbled back at him over the line. 'We've had Inspector Moss on twice trying to contact you.'

'Trouble?' asked Thane quickly.

'He didn't say,' answered MacLeod sadly. 'Just that he's with Doc Williams up at the University, sir. He'd like you to get there.'

'If he phones again, I'm on my way,' said Thane and hung up.

He thanked the switchboard girl, a chubby young brunette who looked as though she should still be at school, and on an impulse left a new message for Cockcroft saying he had to see him urgently.

Then he left and drove the Hillman station wagon hard and fast through the city traffic towards the University. Doc Williams must have come up with something. Gradually, perhaps still mainly blindly, they seemed to be beginning to get towards the truth.

It was a feeling Thane had experienced often enough before. And when that feeling came, with it came the knowledge that every move he made ahead could be vital – bridging past mistakes, avoiding new ones.

Getting at the truth. That was what his job was really all about.

When Glasgow University had been founded back in 1450 the city had been a village. But as the village grew, so did its University till it now sprawled across the rise of grounds called Gilmourhill in a mixture of old and new buildings which dominated a considerable area of the West End skyline.

The Department of Forensic Medicine was a small unit within the rest, vaguely associated with the 'bodysnatchers' in Pathology by non-medical students if they thought about it at all.

But what it lacked in size it more than balanced out in equipment and experience – the equipment by a series of constant budget battles, the experience always in steady supply from the restless city on its doorstep.

When he got there, Thane had no trouble locating Doc Williams. A uniformed attendant took him straight along a corridor past lecture rooms and laboratories which looked more like electronics workshops and finally steered him into a room where the furnishings were more test-tube style.

Doc Williams, in shirt sleeves and with his tie hanging loose, was standing by a laboratory bench talking to an older, taller, skeletally thin figure who wore a white coat and whose expression was close to that of a benevolent vulture. Professor MacMaster ran the Department, had every aspect of its operation at the tips of his bony fingers – and never let Doc Williams forget that the police surgeon had once been among his students.

'Curtain up – you made it, Colin.' Doc Williams spotted him with some relief and beckoned him over. 'We've been waiting for you.'

'Moss seemed to feel you should be a first-hand witness,' said MacMaster. His nostrils flared in a questioning sniff. 'I've no objection to an audience, but frankly it could all have been presented in a written report. In fact, Thane, I imagine you and perhaps even a police surgeon like Williams would understand it better that way, simplified.'

Thane didn't rise to the bait, used to the sparring between the two medical men and MacMaster's derisive views on the average cop's intelligence.

'Where's Phil anyway?' he asked.

'Telephoning,' said Doc Williams. 'We're keeping our fingers crossed till he gets back.'

'For once, I'd almost agree,' mused MacMaster. His face split in a wintery smile. 'Provided Moss doesn't descend to Millside Division's usual and well-known grab-them-by-the-throat standards, his call should clinch matters.'

'Clinch what?' demanded Thane impatiently.

Deliberately, Professor MacMaster turned away and examined an empty test-tube lying on the bench. Doc Williams winked and shook his head.

A full five minutes passed before Moss came into the room but the expression on his face and the spring in his step were enough for MacMaster.

'Agreed?' he asked.

'He says yes.' Moss rubbed his hands and grinned at Thane. 'Sit down and listen.'

'But –'

'Sit down, damn you,' said Moss, still grinning. 'Then shut up, and listen.'

Shrugging, Thane obeyed and took the hard wooden chair Doc Williams pushed towards him.

'Professor?' Moss waved a hand in invitation. 'You start it.'

'Very well.' MacMaster cleared his throat, his manner switching to a clinical precision. 'Thane, you know this Department received certain – ah – tissue and organic samples from the body of this girl Doreen Ashton. My understanding was the cause of death had not been external violence.' His pale blue eyes flickered towards Doc Williams. 'That, of course, would have been better phrased as "apparently not" – but I remember you always did have that weakness, Williams.'

'If I say not, I mean not,' said Williams indignantly. 'Now, look, Professor –'

'Later.' MacMaster was enjoying himself. 'Anyway, the obvious beginning was testing for possible chemical reaction. Suitable – ah – broths were prepared for the sample material as soon as organic disease had been eliminated as a possibility.'

'You decided she'd been poisoned,' paraphrased Thane, tensing. 'But if –'

'Would you prefer my written report?' asked MacMaster, cutting him short.

Fighting for patience, Thane shook his head.

'As I said, chemical tests.' Delicately, MacMaster moistened his lips. 'Now, one fairly standard chemical test is to add sulphuric acid to a solution. We did, and the prepared broth first turned emerald green and then brown. We became interested. When the tube was heated, the colour again changed – this time to violet.' He turned, selected a test-tube from the rack on the bench behind him, and offered it for inspection. 'Violet – and finally this.'

The solution in the test-tube was jet black.

'That reduced the odds in a big way,' explained Doc Williams with a wary eye on MacMaster. 'It meant they knew they were probably working in the strychnos poisons area.'

'Exactly,' purred MacMaster. 'From there, we were involved in elimination – further standard tests,

chemical and electronic.' He paused. 'This department's opinion, for what it may be worth –'

'Hooray,' said Moss in a coarse aside.

'For what it may be worth,' went on MacMaster,
with a glare, 'is that this girl died from strophanthus
poisoning.'

'Strophanthus?' The name meant nothing to Thane.

'Yes. It originated as an African arrow poison,
obtained from the seeds of a species of plant. Though
– ah – in view of the quantity present in her body we
can rule out any Robin Hood type suggestions. Even
remembering the scratches which were found.'

'Thanks,' said Thane bleakly. 'What's left?'

'We reckon she was given it in a drink,' said Doc
Williams, determined to have his share. 'That's the
possibility anyway – there were traces of alcohol in
the stomach.'

'A good possibility.' MacMaster built an expressive
steeple with his long, thin fingers. 'The dosage given
was certainly massive, enough to kill several people.'

'How would it work?' asked Thane, still in
unknown territory.

'Quickly, quite quickly,' assured MacMaster. He
cleared his throat delicately. 'She would collapse, fall
into a coma as the heart action was depressed, and
death would follow rapidly. Medically, of course,
we use the drug to control certain heart conditions
when a patient has reacted badly to digitalis. That's
why I – ah – asked Moss if any of this girl's acquaint-
ances might have had a heart condition. Strophanthus
might have been prescribed.

'Now twist it a little, Colin,' invited Moss. 'Twist it
around in terms of time.'

Suddenly it connected and Thane understood.

'If someone had pills from an old prescription left
over. Say after a death in the family –'

'The MacRath family,' finished Moss. 'It checks out.'

'You're sure?'

'Cast-iron sure.' Moss luxuriated in a low-key belch which made MacMaster wince. 'I've spent the last half-hour tracing the doctor who signed John MacRath's death certificate. All right, MacRath died five years ago – but he died from cardiac disease and he was on strophanthus.'

His mind still in a daze, Thane got to his feet and walked slowly across to stare down at the rack of test-tubes on the bench. Five years – then the same substance which had been used to try to keep one being alive had been the instrument which killed another.

But now they knew. Now they were no longer hunting blindly –

'You'd be amazed how many people keep old medicines in a cupboard,' said MacMaster primly. 'Not – ah – always with any particular purpose in mind, of course. Certainly not murder.'

'Only now and again,' said Doc Williams softly. 'Thanks be for that much, with what's lying around.'

Thane hardly heard them. At last, he had part of what he'd wanted. He knew how Doreen Ashton had died.

But he still didn't know why – except that Victoria MacRath, Mother Bear, had good reason to be making protective noises around her cubs.

Chapter Six

As Friday afternoons went, it was ordinary enough. The sun stayed shining and at the far end of King Street two neds made a smash and grab raid on a jewellery store and ran off with a tray of engagement rings.

A politician made a speech in Millside District Hall, blaming the unions for the latest financial crisis. He attracted three reporters, ten party faithful, and a housewife with a shopping bag who had come thinking the Flower Club was meeting as usual.

Kept off school for the day because she had a cold, a six-year-old girl named Amelia pestered her mother till she was allowed out to buy a comic at the corner newsagent's. On her way back, she was hit by a truck and lost a leg.

There was a fire in a Chinese restaurant. A woman driver lost her temper with a male motorist at traffic lights and reversed hard into his car. The priest at the Episcopalian Church climbed up into the church belfry and discovered that his beadle was running an illicit still.

At the other end of King Street from the jewellery-store raid an old man collapsed and died in his two-roomed house. He lived alone and his body wouldn't be found for another week – when his neighbours would also discover for the first time that he'd been three times decorated for gallantry in World War One.

It was ordinary. Back in his office in Millside Division, Detective Chief Inspector Colin Thane was glad it was staying that way.

A plate with the dried-out remains of some sandwiches lay on the desk in front of him. Phil Moss was draped against his usual filing cabinet beside the Divisional crime map, and both had the air of men who felt they'd run out of things to say. They'd talked, they'd discussed, they'd advised Headquarters. Now the most important thing they had to do was wait until Daniel Cockcroft, solicitor, was finished in court and could tell them what he had against the Glenrath Whisky Investment Corporation.

There were other things happening in the police station though. Down below, in the Olympic Flame's office, the Spanish consul was putting up the necessary bail money to allow the four seamen to be released. The cell next to the seamen was already empty. Two doctors had presented the necessary committal papers to a sheriff in chambers, the order had been signed, and Parrot Savoy had been transferred to an institution where only the doors that mattered stayed locked.

Erickson appeared, back in uniform. He washed down the C.I.D. duty car then began writing up his notes from the morning law class with an air that amounted to a 'Do Not Disturb' sign.

At three-thirty p.m., as the sun came round to strike directly through the window into the crime map, Thane's telephone began ringing.

'Cockcroft?' suggested Moss hopefully, coming to life.

'Too early.' Thane lifted the receiver, answered curtly, and received a surprise. The caller was Robby Deacon.

'I wanted to thank you, sir,' said Deacon happily

over the line. 'After the foul-up I made of things, getting a chance like this is a real surprise.'

'Deacon,' said Thane wearily. 'Exactly what the hell are you going on about?'

'Being back in the Forest Two Hundred. When Duncan MacRath called, I . . .' Deacon faltered with the beginning of doubt. 'Well, I thought it had to be you who told him my car won't be ready. I mean –'

'I don't know a damned thing about it, Deacon,' said Thane. He beckoned Moss, who came over, and lifted the extension earpiece. 'But you'd better tell me – and now.'

'Yes, sir.' Deacon's voice held a flattened, now I've done it again note. 'I'm still at the Training Centre and he phoned me here about ten minutes ago. He – well, he said he'd heard my car was out of the rally and it happens he needs a new co-driver – his brother has a sprained wrist or something. So he offered me the place.'

'And what did you say?' asked Thane sharply.

'I grabbed the chance. Anybody would in the rally game.'

'I suppose they would.' Thane heard Moss mutter a protest in the background and answered it with an uneasy shrug. 'What made you think I'd anything to do with it?'

'I – well, you knew about my car being crocked, sir.' Deacon became almost apologetic. 'But I suppose he must have called round other people in the car club and one of them maybe mentioned it.'

'Probably.' Thane pursed his lips for a moment. 'Deacon, do you know what you're taking on? It will be a strange driver and a strange car. Won't that make it difficult?'

'No problem – we'll use Duncan's pace-notes,' said Deacon confidently. 'I've got my own, but Duncan's are styled to his driving – I'll just be a kind of talking map. It should be quite an experience.'

'No argument there,' admitted Thane grimly. 'When will you meet him?'

'At his place, about eleven tonight – I'm getting a lift out. That gives me a chance to get a few hours' sleep first.' Deacon hesitated. 'This probably isn't a good time to have called you, sir. I mean, with what you've on your plate. But it was just that I thought –'

'Forget it,' said Thane wryly. 'Have a good drive, Robby – and good luck.'

He hung up as Deacon made goodbye noises, sat back with a sigh, and watched Moss replace the extension earpiece on its hook.

'Good luck, Constable Deacon,' mimicked Moss cynically. He perched himself on the edge of the desk and scowled. 'There's just one little item you don't know about, Constable. We may have to arrest your hero before you get to the start line.' A thin finger pointed accusingly to Thane. 'We pick him up while he has a rookie cop in the passenger seat. That's going to look good, isn't it?'

'I could have stopped him, Phil,' admitted Thane. He took a cigarette and sent another rolling across the desk towards Moss. 'It would have been easy enough to put him on extra duty. But remember we'd have risked tipping off the MacRath clan in the process.'

Moss grunted a reluctant agreement and they shared a light. For a moment, Thane smoked in silence. Inviting Deacon to share his rally drive could indicate how secure Duncan MacRath felt about things – or could be a nice piece of window-dressing.

But either way Duncan MacRath was still their front runner. Thane grimaced at the thought, and qualified it deliberately. His story was weak. But by weakness it helped strengthen the possibility that

Victoria MacRath and Peter might have their own secrets to hide.

Even if that tumbled him straight into the old wicked stepmother routine out of fairy-tale land . . .

'We need a couple of search warrants,' said Moss suddenly, cutting across his thoughts. 'One for their office, one for Glenrath House.'

'Get them. But we're not going to use them till we're sure we're ready,' said Thane. 'Relax, Phil – I'm the one supposed to be low on patience around here, remember?'

Moss sighed, came down off the desk, and ambled towards the door.

'Right,' he said solemnly, opening the door. 'I'm asking Headquarters for a transfer – anywhere. My talents are wasted in this fleapit.'

'Go ahead,' grinned Thane. 'Try the Mounted Branch. Maybe they can use an extra mule. Or they might have an opening in the manure business.'

'There's plenty of that around here too,' declared Moss mildly.

He gave a vulgar gesture, chuckled, and wandered off.

Daniel Cockcroft's office finally called at four-thirty. The lawyer was back from court and available till five, when he was due to leave for a golf course. Telling the lawyer's secretary he'd be right over, Thane hung up and was on his way two minutes later.

It was warm and bright and pleasant as he drove in towards the city centre. Another time, and he might have noticed more of the girls in summer dresses or the way the sun picked out the new high-rise blocks among the mellowed grime of the city's older silhouette.

But his thoughts stayed ahead, with Cockcroft. Like most Scottish solicitors, he was usually close-mouthed when it came to gossiping about clients' business. So Daniel Cockcroft must be angry, really angry about something.

Thane hoped it was that way. Then he'd be more likely to get what he wanted without it first having to be filtered through a defensive barrier of noises about legal ethics.

It took fifteen minutes to get to the lawyer's office and the reception when he arrived was reasonably encouraging. He was shown straight through into Daniel Cockcroft's room and the lawyer, a small, fat butter-ball of a man with rimless glasses and receding hair, came out from behind his desk to greet him.

'I don't think we've had you visit here before, Chief Inspector.' Cockcroft gave him a moist but firm hand-shake, dismissed his secretary with a wave, and gestured to a chair already waiting beside the desk. 'Sit down – tell me what I can do for you.'

Thane sat, waited until the little man was settled in his own place again, and knew the eyes behind those rimless glasses were studying him with considerable care.

'I was round earlier,' he began.

'And I was in court.' Cockcroft sighed, sat back, and shoved his hands into the pockets of his pin-stripe jacket. 'A young idiot on two charges of theft – a sheriff and jury case. We got away with the good old Scottish verdict of not proven. I think they really meant go away and don't do it again – and thank God I made him get a real haircut and buy a decent suit. That helped a lot.'

'Then you've had a good day,' said Thane dryly.

'Reasonable.' Cockcroft nodded contentedly. 'Then I came back to your message, Chief Inspector. My curiosity has been growing ever since.'

145

'Good.' Thane forgot the cautious, probing approaches he'd thought of on the way over and decided to go straight in. 'I came to ask what you could tell me about a firm called Glenrath.'

Cockcroft's face showed a twitch of surprise. He rubbed his chin with a hand which had a heavy gold ring on the wedding finger and whistled silently to himself for a moment.

'Getting straight to the point, aren't you?' he said at last.

'I'm fairly low on options,' countered Thane. 'You're supposed to have been saying that you wouldn't trust the Glenrath outfit further than you could throw them.'

'Then it seems I've been saying too much too loudly,' mused Cockcroft, frowning. 'What's your interest, Chief Inspector?'

'A murder.'

'I see. Well, I'm not too surprised. I read the papers.' The man's pudgy hands reached for a box of paperclips on his desk. Slowly, carefully, he began threading them into a chain. Then, without looking up, he asked, 'You think there's a connection with – well, my possible problems?'

'Everything shapes that way.' Thane watched the chain gain a few more clips. 'I'm short of a motive.'

'Which you think I might supply?' Cockcroft sighed and let the chain slide between his fingers back into the box. 'The matter involves a client.'

'Damn your client,' said Thane wearily. 'We're talking about a murder –'

Cockcroft stopped him with a protesting hand. 'I was going to say the matter involves a client whose best interests might be served by talking to you.' He smiled at Thane's expression. 'In fact, in the circumstances I'd be a fool if I didn't take the chance.'

He got up, went over to a filing cabinet, and returned with a thick file of papers which he laid carefully on the desk.

'The estate of the late Hannah Elizabeth Tucker, widow of this parish, who died a few weeks ago at the quite respectable age of eighty-six,' he said dryly. 'Mourned by her relatives, of course. She left about two hundred thousand pounds in her will – the late Mr Tucker made his money selling an obscure and nasty brand of low cost pet food.'

'You're acting for the relatives?' queried Thane.

'For the family generally,' confirmed Cockcroft. 'I was the old girl's lawyer for years, though that didn't amount to much. She lived alone and quietly – wanted it that way. Usually she told me to keep my damned nose out of her business.'

He opened the file, shuffled the papers slowly, and drew out one sheet with a sigh. Still holding it, he shook his head unhappily.

'Thane, I've a confession to make. I should have noticed something about Hannah Tucker the last few times I saw her – or maybe I did, but didn't pay enough attention. She was an intelligent woman but her age had begun to catch up on her.'

'It happens,' agreed Thane. 'Physically or her mind?'

'Her mind.' Cockcroft sucked his teeth in an angry way. 'I know now that over the last couple of years she'd become more and more confused and forgetful. It's a common enough pattern – but like a fool I didn't spot it.'

'And?'

'This first.' Cockcroft gave him the sheet of paper. 'A listing of Hannah Tucker's principal investments – or what they were supposed to be.'

Thane skimmed his way down the typewritten columns then stopped and read one line again, shaping a whistle. According to the list, Hannah Tucker at death had had a total of sixty thousand pounds invested in bulk whisky through the Glenrath Corporation. It was by far the largest single item, the rest being a scatter of gilt-edged and industrial shares.

'Who advised her on investments?' he asked neutrally.

'She did her own homework,' answered Cockcroft. 'Did it well too. I know experts who would charge a fat fee and still recommend that kind of portfolio. Hannah Tucker made up her mind years ago, bought, and that was that.'

Brakes screeched outside in the street then came a furious blaring of angry car-horns. The sounds were like an irrelevant intrusion in the drab, dusty room with its old, bound law books, the untidy bundles of paper tied with pink tape and the sepia-tinted photographs of previous generations of solicitors who had founded the firm. There were other office rooms like it in plenty – rooms where past met present and so often decided future.

'What happened?' asked Thane. He waited, knowing that men like Cockcroft couldn't be rushed, that each word was weighed and chosen with care.

'When Hannah Tucker died and I became executor there didn't seem to be many problems,' said Cockcroft at last. 'Her will amounted to a few small legacies to charities and the bulk to be divided between the family. So I started gathering things together.'

'And the trouble started?'

Cockcroft nodded. 'I went to her house – the first time I'd been, Thane. She always came here.' One pudgy arm gestured helplessly. 'You should have seen that house. Right at the start we found a coffee-pot in the kitchen crammed full of cash. We found money stuffed in drawers, more money under the carpets, a bundle of dividend slips she hadn't bothered to take to the bank were jammed in behind a clock. In one hour we collected two thousand pounds that way – if the house had ever been burgled your people wouldn't have known where to begin.'

Thane made no comment but he knew what Cockcroft meant. It was only ten days since an old tramp, sleeping rough, had been brought into Millside station on a drunk and disorderly charge. While he was being deloused and generally cleaned over a thousand pounds had been found sewn into the lining of his coat – yet he'd been suffering from malnutrition.

'People.' Cockcroft scowled at the world in general. 'Anyway, we got the house straightened out. Then I tackled the investment portfolio – I sent the usual letter advising that I was acting as executor and asked for a confirmation of holding. Routine again, except for the reply I got from Glenrath.'

He delved into the file, muttered his way through a batch of correspondence, then found the one he wanted.

'Here's their reply. According to them, Hannah Tucker's holding was down to thirty-five thousand pounds.'

Twenty-five thousand pounds down – silently, his mouth suddenly dry, Thane took the letter and read the curt, formal wording. The signature at the foot was Duncan MacRath, the letter was a month old.

'That's your start-line,' said Cockcroft heavily. 'I phoned first, to ask if they'd made a mistake. Then I visited, wrote them, visited again – and gave up a week ago after a final row in their office.' The small, fat solicitor shook his head despairingly. 'Their story is that over the past three years Hannah Tucker had been drawing almost ten thousand a year from her funds – and always demanding cash. They've got signed and dated receipts to account for every penny.'

'But you don't believe it?' asked Thane bluntly.

'I deal in facts.' Cockcroft's struggling restraint was more effective than any purpled outburst. 'The old girl probably didn't spend much more in a week than she drew in Government pension. The house was littered with money – but not that kind of money, Thane. So what the hell did she do with twenty-five thousand in cash?'

'I've never had that kind of problem,' said Thane dryly. 'Ordinarily, my guess would be that there was a happy bookie somewhere.'

'Old Hannah thought gambling sinful,' said Cockcroft curtly. 'She fired her last housekeeper years ago because she caught her sneaking out to Bingo.'

Thane shrugged and deliberately whittled at another possibility.

'Tax evasion? She could have farmed it out to the family to beat death duties.' Any sane Scot studied ways of trying to score over the taxation system – and if they were caught the main reaction, even in the most upright circles, came down to the verdict that they should have been more careful.

'No.' Cockcroft glowered morosely through his spectacles. 'I checked round the family and any friends she had left. They all say they were lucky if they got as much as a pair of socks from her at Christmas – and now they're jumping up and down asking where the hell the money went.'

'Great expectations unstuck?' Thane gave a soft chuckle. The rest of Hannah Tucker's estate would have seemed a small fortune to most people.

Cockcroft wasn't amused. 'Thane, either she was giving away bundles of money in the street or –' he paused, inbred caution taking over – 'or you can draw your own conclusions.'

'You said they produced receipts,' mused Thane.

'First thing I'd want to know would be if they were authentic.'

'A first year law student would have thought of that one,' snapped the fat little man. 'They showed me the receipts, all legally competent, signed and dated over postage stamps. I persuaded them to let me have the lot on loan – the story was I wanted to satisfy the family.' His mouth tightened. 'Two handwriting experts I use on court work spent days comparing those receipts against samples of Hannah Tucker's signature from my own files. Both gave the same answer – all the signatures were genuine.'

'And that's when you gave up?'

'Yes – and no. I gave them back the receipts, though I kept photocopies. In law, I hadn't a leg to stand on – not against her kind of background. Anyway, Glenrath have a whiter than white image in the business world. But –'

'Well?'

Instead of answering, Cockcroft swung round, crossed to a cabinet, produced a bottle of whisky and glasses, and poured two generous measures. He brought the drinks over and gave one to Thane.

'Against my usual rule,' he said grimly. 'I don't believe in drinking during office hours. But when I think of this business, I need it.'

Thane raised his glass in a silent toast, sipped, and watched Cockcroft demolish about half his drink in a single gulp.

'Call it medicinal.' Cockcroft sighed and sucked his lips. 'I'll tell you what I did, Thane. I made a few inquiries of my own around some of my friends in the legal game – and I discovered I wasn't alone. At least two other law firms in this city have had the same experience. They've had old women die and leave money invested in Glenrath – and had an unpleasant surprise when it came to asking about settlement.' He took another swallow of whisky. 'I'm a mild man by nature. But every time I think about what's probably going on I could go and damned well strangle Peter MacRath.'

'Peter?' Thane didn't attempt to hide his surprise. 'I thought you were dealing with Duncan MacRath.'

'Only on first contact, then the other one took over. They each handle their own lists of clients.' Cockcroft twisted a humourless smile. 'That's the story. There's not a thing anyone can do about it – make any kind of public noise and I could be sued into the ground for slander.'

Thane eyed him quizzically. 'But you reckon they're milking some of their accounts?'

'Did I say that?' Cockcroft twitched an expressive eyebrow. 'You wanted facts and I've given you them. That's all.'

'Then let's avoid the legal-style quibbling,' said Thane wearily. 'Suppose some firm we won't name set out to milk clients' accounts in the way we're thinking about. How would they do it?'

'Some fictional firm?' Cockcroft's manner eased. 'It would be easy enough. They'd keep tabs on a few likely candidates then go along at the right time and say they'd some papers which had to be signed. First time, it would be some meaningless document while they made friends with their candidate and checked the ground. After that –' he slammed his glass on the desk – 'in for the kill.'

'You make it sound pretty easy,' said Thane warily, his own thoughts racing ahead.

'Easy?' Cockcroft shrugged. 'Believe me, the old girls would be so chirpy at having a visitor they'd scribble their signatures on anything – and forget it had even happened by bedtime.' He smiled dryly at Thane's lingering disbelief. 'Look, I have clients in here every day who'll sign whatever I stick under their noses. They don't bother reading the words – and I'm talking about allegedly intelligent business-men in their prime.'

Thane nodded and sat silent. All there was left to presume was that Doreen Ashton, as the MacRaths' secretary, had stumbled across some flaw in the scheme. Then, after her own private crisis of decision, she'd decided to contact the police – contact him.

Once again he found himself cursing that ill chance. But now it was against the memory of the other telephone number they'd found in the dead girl's clothing.

Had she changed her mind again and decided to confide in someone else she thought she could trust . . . the petite, precise Victoria MacRath?

Mother Bear, with her cubs in danger. If Duncan and Peter were both in the scheme the options were confused from there on. But Hannah Tucker had been Peter MacRath's client – and his alibi over the time of the murder rested squarely on his mother. His natural mother.

Thane moistened his lips. 'You say you know two other law firms who've had the same trouble with Glenrath. Who were they dealing with?'

'Peter – the fair-haired one.' Daniel Cockcroft con-sidered Thane's face wisely. 'And you said murder, Thane. Is – well, is he the man?'

'What kind of a question is that for a lawyer to ask a cop?' queried Thane dryly.

He got a little of his own back in the process. But it was a good question, and the answer had firmed.

When he left the law office five minutes later, Thane had the Glenrath documents, including the photostats of the receipts signed by Hannah Tucker, in an enve-lope under one arm.

Cockcroft's parting words stayed with him.

'You're out to nail a killer. But in my book, robbing confused old women runs a close second – because we all get old, Thane. That's what I forgot and that's my share of the blame.'

Just as he hadn't worried too much about a missed telephone call. But that, at least, was an account he could try to square.

The home-bound rush hour traffic was at its peak as Colin Thane drove back through the sun-lit streets to Millside. He reached the police office, parked his station wagon in the wire-fenced compound, and went straight up to the C.I.D. area.

He was surprised to find Phil Moss wasn't in sight. But Sergeant MacLeod bustled over to meet him, his broad face worried.

'Where's Inspector Moss?' asked Thane, sensing trouble.

'At Headquarters, sir.' MacLeod kept his voice low, almost conspiratorial, and Thane realized the other C.I.D. men around were watching from their desks. 'Chief Superintendent Ilford phoned, looking for you – and he took the call.'

'Then what?' Thane was puzzled.

MacLeod shrugged dourly. 'He didn't tell me, sir. He just said Mr Ilford wanted him over there, straight away – and that you were to go there too, the moment you got back.'

'Nothing more?'

'Nothing.' MacLeod shook his head. 'But – ah – he didn't look too happy about it, sir.'

Thane thanked him and went back the way he'd come.

Fifteen minutes later he knocked on the city C.I.D. boss's office door. The signal light spat a quick 'enter'

154

signal, he went in, and even as he closed the door again he felt a tension in the air.

Buddha Ilford sat stony-faced behind his desk, arms folded, his massive shoulders hunched forward, chin almost on his chest, his mouth a tight, uncompromising line. For a moment Thane thought Ilford was alone, then he realized Phil Moss stood by the window. Thin face slightly flushed, hands thrust deep in his pockets, Moss gave him a fractional nod but said nothing.

'You came,' said Ilford grimly. 'Thanks – thanks very much.' The sarcasm behind the words stabbed home. 'Now perhaps I'll get some answers. Better than I've been able to get so far.'

Thane glanced at Moss, who shrugged wryly.

'Any answers you want, sir,' said Thane in an even voice. The envelope with Hannah Tucker's estate papers suddenly felt very comforting under his arm. 'The question should have come to me anyway – not Phil.'

'Protocol?' Ilford snarled the word. 'Thane, you applied for two search warrants – for the Glenrath office and Victoria MacRath's house. I heard, I tried to find out why – and all I've got so far from Moss is that you were out seeing some damned lawyer and couldn't be contacted.'

'What I said was I thought you should wait,' corrected Moss mildly.

'Wait?' Ilford glared at him. 'Do either of you know the size of explosion that would follow if you went trampling in without cast-iron reason? Thane, you're not dealing with backstreet neds. The MacRaths are – are –'

'Respectable?' suggested Thane grimly.

'Something more important. They're in the investment world.' Ilford reddened but kept on. 'All right, you know I've got money in their whisky. I'm small-time compared with the people I'm thinking about – but if you did this and it went wrong then you'd be wasting your time apologizing afterwards. You'd be in deeper trouble than you ever dreamed existed.'

'Money always matters,' murmured Moss.

'That's only part of what I'm talking about.' Ilford slammed a fist on the desk. 'Look, I know about the new post-mortem results. I know about that heart drug. But we need a hell of a sight more before we talk about search warrants.'

'We've got it,' said Thane quietly. He laid the envelope in the desk. 'It's in there.'

Ilford froze, staring at him. Then he grabbed the envelope, spilled the contents out, and began reading. Gradually his rage subsided and puzzlement took its place. At last, he looked up.

'What the hell is this all about?' he asked warily.

Thane told him. Midway through, Ilford reached for his pipe, filled it, and lit it without letting his concentration lapse for a moment.

At the finish he gave a long sigh and gave a nod which held only a remnant of doubt.

'All right, you've convinced me,' he said wearily. 'But there are still holes in it all – damned big ones. Didn't the housekeeper say Victoria and Peter were both at home that night?'

'Not exactly.' Moss answered him, easing round to get beside Thane. 'She said they were both there when she went out and that she said goodnight to Victoria when she got back. She just – well, presumed Peter was there too.' He paused then added ruefully. 'So did we, because Victoria said so.'

Ilford cursed quietly. 'And Duncan MacRath?'

'Maybe he was in on it, maybe he wasn't – that's another of our gaps,' said Thane wryly. 'Right now, I wouldn't gamble either way.'

'And young Robby Deacon is driving with him.' Ilford found his pipe had gone out and needed two matches to get it going again, his face worried and thoughtful all the time. 'Well, maybe that helps in some ways.' He made up his mind. 'All right, we go in tonight as far as the office is concerned, then take it from there. But we wait till the place is empty. Finding what we want could take time.'

'We've a couple of men watching it now,' murmured Moss. He gave Thane a sideways glance. 'It seemed a reasonable notion. I – uh – forgot to mention it before.'

Thane grinned. 'Anything else you forgot?'

Moss shook his head. 'Nothing. But I had Doreen Ashton's relatives in. They're nice people, which didn't make it easier.'

Ilford cleared his throat heavily and quickly.

'Let's get this set up,' he said curtly. 'And someone better have a damned big chopping block handy if we're wrong – a whole line of heads are going to be on it.'

The two plain-clothes men on watch outside the Glenrath Whisky Investment Corporation's office were meticulous in their reports.

By five-thirty all the staff appeared to have left. Ten minutes later Duncan MacRath walked out, climbed into his Ford rally car, and drove away. One of the watchers went up to the Glenrath floor and found the office door locked. But a light was still burning on the other side of the frosted glass so he came back down again ... and twenty minutes later Peter MacRath left the building and departed in his car.

Following orders, the plain-clothes men waited another half-hour. By six-thirty, the entire office block seemed deserted and likely to stay that way. The building janitor appeared and began to lock the main door, ready to leave for the night. Stopping him, the plain-clothes men took the man back into his cubicle and used the telephone there.

Five minutes later, their cars parked discreetly round the next corner, the C.I.D. search team arrived on foot. Ilford was there with a broad-shouldered, tanned man who looked like a professional footballer but who in fact was a Headquarters detective inspector and an accountancy expert. Thane brought his own team – Phil Moss carrying the search warrant, MacLeod and Beech, and Erickson who had asked if he could come along. The big, blond driver reckoned he might get some good background for a law class thesis that was coming up.

The janitor had spare keys to the Glenrath office door and let them in. Then he went down again to his cubicle with Beech as an escort. And the others got to work.

At first it was a quiet, easy-going process. A prowl through the silent rooms, past typewriters under dust-covers, tidied desks and waste-baskets waiting the cleaners who would come to empty them. There were unwashed coffee cups in a sink in the women's powder room. A pile of stencilled circulars lay ready to be put in envelopes when Monday came round.

'Got the geography?' asked Ilford at last. He got his answer from the faces around and nodded. 'Then get started.'

The cabinets in the file room were locked but Sergeant MacLeod had a bundle of master-keys – and where these failed Erickson was there with a slim, beautifully engineered jemmy. The original owner was doing five years, but he hadn't had any kind of warrant when he was caught using it.

Thane and Moss concentrated on the MacRaths' personal offices. Ilford prowled in general at first then

158

settled at a desk in the outer office, waiting, watching as the Headquarters accountancy expert began accumulating a small mountain of books and ledgers.

Towards the end of the first half-hour they found Hannah Tucker's file in one of the cabinets. Ilford and the Headquarters man went into a huddle over it, then Ilford brought the file across to Thane.

'These are your originals.' An uneasy flicker of doubt back in his voice, he fanned a handful of receipt forms. 'All signed and dated – and the rest of the paperwork seems to back them up.'

'That's how we expected it.' Thane glanced past him to where the Headquarters man was already hunched over another account book. 'What does he say?'

'Nothing – his kind never do till they're sure.' Ilford made it one stage short of outright condemnation and grimly tucked the sheets back in the file. 'Stay with him. I'm going to take this lot over to the Scientific Bureau and turn them loose on it.'

He left, they stayed, and time dragged by. There were two safes in the office and a telephone call brought another man round from Headquarters who had spent a lifetime at his particular speciality. He brought more keys and a tiny, tool-roll along, opened the larger of the two safes in under a minute, and need only ten minutes perseverance to master the second.

The total yield was the Glenrath petty cash box, some old ledgers, and a spare set of keys for the cabinets they'd already opened. The safe expert departed, making mumbling noises about his time having been wasted.

They drew the office blinds at dusk and switched on the lights. At eleven, Thane sent Erickson out to find coffee and sandwiches. Then he phoned the Scientific Bureau, but Buddha Ilford wasn't there.

159

'He had us play around with those receipt forms for a spell,' said the cheerful duty officer at the other end of the line. 'Then he grabbed them all and said something about going off to a hospital. Don't ask me why – he wasn't being particularly talkative.'

'Did you get anywhere with the stuff?' asked Thane, puzzled.

'No.' The duty officer was casual, long used to divisional men who thought there was nothing else in life but their own particular case of the moment. 'But it still looks like you can forget forgery – and the typed wording hasn't been altered after signature, if that's what you had in mind.'

Thane thanked him and hung up, cursing Ilford for his disappearing act and wondering what devious scheme the C.I.D. chief had in mind. Phil Moss was helping the Headquarters accountancy man sort out ledgers into carefully designated piles and he talked towards them.

'Getting anywhere?' he asked.

'Just sorting out what I want to take away,' said the Headquarters man vaguely. 'You can't rush this sort of thing, Chief Inspector.'

Erickson came back with a parcel of greasy bacon sandwiches and cartons of coffee. They took a break, scattered around the desk in Doreen Ashton's office, and were finishing the sandwiches when Ilford returned.

He was grinning from ear to ear like an overgrown schoolboy and the Hannah Tucker file was under his arm.

'Any of that coffee left?' he demanded happily. 'I've earned it. And Thane, you can forget about your head being on any chopping block. You were right!'

Thane scrambled to his feet and stared at him. Moss muttered what might have been a prayer of thanks

160

through a final mouthful of bacon. Then, as Ilford stood grinning, the group of men gathered round him.

'Any notion where I've been?' he asked.

'Scientific Bureau said a hospital.' Thane didn't try to hide his bewilderment.

'That's right.' Ilford settled in the chair Sergeant MacLeod brought over, folded his arms and took his time. 'I had those damned receipts X-rayed.' He enjoyed their blank reaction. 'What the hell do any of you use for memories? Don't you remember a County case about a faked will a few years back?'

'Watermarks,' said Erickson suddenly. 'I had a law class lecture about the case.'

'Thank you, Constable Erickson,' said Ilford sardonically. 'I'm glad it makes sense to somebody. How about telling your Chief Inspector what I mean?'

Erickson's face made it plain he wished he'd kept his mouth shut.

'The will was signed over a postage stamp, sir,' he said warily. 'I – uh – well, I know the watermark and weave of paper in the stamp were wrong. That's about all I remember.'

'It's enough.' Ilford sucked his lips for a moment. 'What about that coffee?'

Scowling his impatience, Moss brought over a paper cup. Sipping it, Ilford gave a sigh of satisfaction. 'All right, the will case. They broke that by X-raying the postage stamp on the will – the signature and date were across the stamp, like on any Scottish legal document. Except all British postage stamps had a watermark then, and the watermark happened to be for a stamp issue that didn't come out for a year after the will was supposed to have been signed.'

Thane nodded, remembering. Until the County case, everyone from Scotland Yard to Post Office experts had said it was impossible to identify the watermark on a stamp after it had been stuck on any

161

kind of document. But a Glasgow hospital radio-grapher named Dan Graham had juggled around with X-rays and filters and done it. He had also produced proof that the weave of paper on any print-run of stamps was almost as good as a watermark and as individual as any signature.

'Like I said, I went to a hospital.' Ilford put a hand into a file and brought out half a dozen photoprints. 'The Post Office don't bother having a watermark in stamps any more. But there's still the weave of paper from which they're printed. So we take the stamps from your receipts, Thane – supposed to be spread over three years. The X-ray boys found they all showed the same paperweave, one the Post Office says belongs to a run of stamps that came out less than a year ago.'

'Can I see one?' Moss reached out with a hand still greasy from the bacon sandwiches.

'Not till you wipe your fingers,' said Ilford coldly.

Shrugging, Moss wandered over to the waste bas-ket, lifted out a crumpled sheet of paper, and used it to rub his hands.

'Then it wasn't done the way we thought,' Thane said thoughtfully, peering at the prints.

'But still near enough to it,' emphasized Ilford. 'Peter MacRath didn't move in till late on – but he spread the receipts back on the instalment plan, and conned old Hannah Tucker into dating them the way he wanted.'

'It's happened before, it'll happen again,' said the Headquarters accountancy man dryly. 'But it will be interesting to see how he juggled the books to match.'

'If he didn't do it in advance.' Ilford stopped and gave an irritated scowl in Phil Moss's direction.

Moss wasn't listening to them. Instead his whole attention was focused on the crumpled paper he'd used to wipe the grease from his fingers – paper he was now carefully smoothing flat on the desk.

'Am I boring you?' asked Ilford brusquely.

Moss shook his head absently then slouched straight across to Thane.

'Take a look,' he invited.

Thane took the grease-stained sheet, saw three lines of typing with the third line incomplete, and looked up sharply.

'Any more of this?'

Moss shook his head again, his eyes hard. 'And I noticed that bucket was empty last time we were here.'

'What's wrong?' Impatiently, Ilford joined them and scowled at the typewritten lines. 'VSL, S500R, FR –' he stopped, then demanded – 'what kind of gibberish is that?'

'Pace-note coding,' said Thane in a quiet, deliberately controlled voice which masked a sudden feeling of sick foreboding. 'Rally drivers use it – they make up their own driving codes for a route.'

Or as Robby Deacon had described it so graphically, a talking map.

'Coding? What kind of coding?' Ilford still didn't understand.

'You could almost blindfold Duncan MacRath tonight and he would still be able to drive,' said Moss with an acid patience. 'He does what the pace-notes tell him, whether it's setting up a car for a bend, going flat out, or braking. He obeys the pace-notes – and to hell with whether he can see what's ahead.'

'Absolute trust.' Ilford realized now and his broad face became grave. 'Who had these notes, Thane?'

'Peter MacRath – but now he has called off, Robby Deacon gets the job tonight.'

'And who typed the originals?'

163

'Doreen Ashton.' Thane gestured at the typewriter on the desk. 'Probably on that same machine.'

'Then it just happens that Peter works late tonight,' said Moss in a flat, unemotional voice. 'Suppose he typed just one substitute page with a single alteration – like an L instead of an R. Left bend instead of right.'

Thane gave a silent nod, mentally picturing the scene. A car with headlights blazing, going flat out through the dark tunnel of a forest track. Robby Deacon in the navigation seat, reading the route by the light of a tiny, shielded lamp. Duncan MacRath, out to win, obeying every carefully decided instruction regardless of what instinct might tell him. Every instruction . . . when one altered symbol could mean disaster.

'The bastard,' said Ilford almost disbelievingly, staring at the crumpled, greasy sheet of paper.

'Looks like his typing came unstuck first try,' said the Headquarters accountancy man lugubriously. 'Then he forgot afterwards.'

'Which makes him a careless bastard for once – thank God.' Ilford came to life again. 'When does this rally start?'

'The first car leaves at midnight.' Thane glanced at his watch and winced – that was only ten minutes away.

'Then try Glenrath House,' snarled Ilford. 'You do it, Moss. Get hold of Deacon, tell him to keep Duncan MacRath there. I don't give a damn about the rest of it for now – as long as we stop them.'

Moss was already on his way to the switchboard in the outer office. He came back in two minutes.

'They've already gone – Deacon, the MacRaths, even Victoria,' he reported bleakly. 'The housekeeper says they left twenty minutes ago.' He shook his head, anticipating the next question. 'There's no way we can contact the start point. It's in the middle of the forest.'

164

Buddha Ilford's heavy, thick-set face had greyed. But the authority in his voice cracked over them like a whiplash. 'Erickson.'

'Sir?' The big, blond duty driver could anticipate what was coming.

'Get your car out there fast – like you had Jackie Stewart at his best on your tail. Thane, you and Moss go with him. I'll contact the County force to send any unit they've got anywhere near.' Ilford drew a deep breath. 'Now move – just get there.'

They were already on their way as he hurried through to the telephone at the switchboard.

Chapter Seven

It was the start of a nightmare of driving Colin Thane would never forget – a high-speed nightmare dominated by the way Erickson used every trick of his pursuit driver's training as they raced through the night towards the forests and the rally start-point at Drymen.

He sat hunched over the steering wheel, the Millside car siren wailing and blue roof-light flashing. Other traffic wavered or scattered from their path while the car weaved and skidded and never slowed. In the dim glow from the facia the instrument needles jerked and wavered while the big V12 power unit roared and howled, carburettors gobbling air, gears screaming.

And always the big, blond driver was in absolute control – mastering one situation, already setting up his car for the next ahead.

For Thane and Moss, it was a time to stay silent. Up front, Thane had the seat belt harness to keep him in place. In the rear, Moss was thrown around on corners and gave an occasional soft grunt of suppressed alarm as yet another truck or bus or startled car-driver appeared momentarily ahead then vanished, lost somewhere back in the snarling rasp of the car's four-branch exhaust.

The city vanished behind them, their headlamp beams lanced the darkness ahead and, the siren still wailing, they built up more and more speed – while Erickson, face impassive, something close to a smile on his lips, began a strange humming sound which finally sank home to Thane as the tune of an old, wonderfully obscene North-East Scottish bothy ballad.

The eighteen mile distance blurred. Tiny, white-washed cottages, cattle huddled against a fence, an open-mouthed tramp pushing a bicycle – all were mere punctuation marks briefly caught and lost in the headlights.

They reached Drymen, the village passed in a slightly longer blur, and they were in the forest land. There, at last, they had to slow and Erickson ceased his humming as he fought the Millside car on over the narrow, disintegrating road surface. The wooden bridge rattled loudly as they crossed, they raced on through a black funnel of trees – then, suddenly, they were at the start-line clearing and skidding to a halt.

Thane tumbled out, Moss at his heels. There were cars and people all around. A County car, blue roof-lamp still winking, one door lying open and a message coming in over its radio, lay just ahead. Another County car was broadside across the Forest Two Hundred start line. Puzzled, indignant voices shouted and a miniature wave of figures hurried towards them.

A red-faced County sergeant got to Thane first.

'MacRath was fourth car off, sir – ten minutes ahead of us getting here,' he reported unhappily. Glancing over his shoulder at their irate audience of rally crews in sheepskin jackets, anoraks and assorted headgear, he added grimly, 'We stopped the rest o' them, and they're not liking it. I've told them why, but –'

'Told us some crazy story about Duncan being in danger,' wrathfully interrupted a big, beefy man who wore an official's armband. 'I don't know who the hell you are, but I want to know what's really going on.'

Thane ignored him. 'Sergeant, what about Peter MacRath?'

'Gone too,' said the County man bitterly. 'But Mrs MacRath is still here. She's over at the secretary's tent.'

The beefy man with the armband began protesting again and tugged at Thane's arm. Thane brushed him aside.

'Phil –' he beckoned Moss nearer – 'get some sense into these people. And find someone who has any kind of notion about these pace-notes.'

Moss gave a quick grunt of understanding, pushed himself between Thane and the beefy man, and began talking earnestly while the rally contestants gathered round him. Shoving past, Thane hurried across the car-littered clearing to the tent the County sergeant had indicated.

Victoria MacRath was standing at the entrance to the tent, her small, slight figure framed in the bright glow of a kerosene lamp. She wore a heavy wool sweater and trousers and she waited on him coming, her thin face pale but her manner still defiant.

'I presume you're responsible for all this?' She gestured curtly towards the confusion at the start line. 'As for this stupid story about Duncan –'

'Stupid?' Savagely, Thane cut her short. 'Stop playing games, Victoria. He's only your stepson – but do you really want him dead?'

The sheer vehemence behind his words made her waver. The grey eyes stared at him for a long moment of disbelief, then showed something close to speechless horror.

'You don't know what you're saying.' Her voice wavered irresolutely.

168

'I know your fair-haired darling Peter altered Duncan's pace-notes,' rasped Thane. He scowled at an approaching official and sent him into headlong retreat. 'Now I'm asking, Victoria. Did he tell you?'

She shook her head dumbly.

'But you covered up for Peter when he killed Doreen Ashton, didn't you?' went on Thane relentlessly. 'And that was to stop her talking.' He took a half-step nearer. 'You knew that part, didn't you?'

Victoria MacRath seemed to age as he watched. Her mouth trembled.

'I knew,' she admitted in a tired, resigned voice. 'But only afterwards. Peter told me and – well, I tried to help him. But you've got to believe that I wouldn't have let Duncan be blamed in his place.'

'That's for later,' he said curtly. 'Where is Peter?'

'He said he was going to drive over to the halfway control.' Her hands made a small, helpless gesture. 'He – he said he'd give Duncan a cheer as he went through.'

Thane swore under his breath. 'Can he drive with that strapped-up wrist?'

She nodded. 'He drove me here. He – well, he said he probably could have gone with Duncan but that he didn't want to disappoint Robby Deacon at the last minute.'

'I'll bet,' said Thane bitterly. Then he turned as Moss came running towards them.

'We've got the place more or less pin-pointed,' said Moss breathlessly. 'Some of these drivers checked the sheet we found against their own pace-notes.'

'How bad is it?' asked Thane.

'Bad enough.' Moss paused and glanced significantly at Victoria MacRath.

'Spell it out,' said Thane bleakly.

'There's a fake right turn that takes him off the route on one of the fast special stages.' Moss sucked his lips.

'Then if the map's accurate, he's in trouble. There's a long straight and he'll expect a fast right turn again at the end. Except the damned road goes left.'

Beside them, Victoria MacRath gave a muffled sound like a sob. Thane ignored her.

'How far from here?' he asked.

'About fifty miles as he's going,' said Moss. 'There's just a chance of a possible shorter route over the hills and some of the rally people are trying to work it out now. Oh – and Deacon brought a fan club along. Kate Manson and a car load of rookies from the Training Centre are here.'

'Just keep them out of the way and hurry those map readers.' Thane changed his mind. 'No, tell the Manson girl I need her.'

Moss nodded and hurried off again towards the cluster of cars. Turning, Thane found Victoria MacRath was staring out into the black night beyond the clearing.

'Any doubts left now?' he asked flatly.

'No.' She gave a quick headshake and faced him earnestly. 'You'll try, won't you? Try to stop Duncan, I mean?'

'Yes. But we'll still want Peter for murder,' he said brutally and saw her wince. 'Did Peter tell you his sideline, Victoria? How he'd been robbing old women?'

'Afterwards. He told me everything afterwards,' she said wearily. 'He'd taken money before – only small sums, when I made good the money and Duncan never knew. But this time – well, even Peter knew there was too much involved and that I couldn't have done anything.'

'What was it?' asked Thane bluntly. 'Gambling?'

'Mainly.'

'And Doreen Ashton?' Out of the corner of his eyes he saw Kate Manson and signalled her to stay back.

'She found out.' Victoria MacRath's sigh was lost in the soft background hiss of the kerosene lamp. 'That evening, she telephoned me at home – just as you guessed. She said she had to see me urgently and privately – and that it concerned Peter.' She closed her eyes a moment, recalling a nightmare. 'The girl told me she had to help Duncan with the rally work party and – well, I arranged to meet her when she got back to Glasgow.'

'Where?'

'She said she'd get a lift back to Leyland Street. I promised I'd wait for her in my car near there.'

'But Peter went instead,' said Thane grimly.

She nodded. 'In my car.'

'Why?'

'Because he was in the house and heard the end of the call.' The woman paused and shrugged. 'I asked him what it was all about and – and he laughed. He said he'd been dating the girl and they'd had a row but that if he went he could calm her down.'

'And you believed him?'

'I wanted to.' She made it a simple statement of fact.

'Go on,' he said quietly. 'Peter went – and then?'

'Then I waited till our housekeeper got back before I went to bed. I intended to stay awake but –' she sighed briefly – 'as you get older you tire more easily. I fell asleep. The next thing I knew was Peter wakening me. It was two a.m.'

'That's when he told you?' asked Thane softly.

She nodded. 'He said they'd quarrelled in the car. The girl had found out what he was doing and – well, she was going to the police.'

'So he killed her.'

'Peter said he didn't mean to do it,' she said with a dull desperation. 'But they struggled and – and it just happened. So he hid her body and tried to make things look as if she'd been attacked by a prowler.'

171

A large, furry-bodied moth came out of the darkness and began fluttering around the kerosene lamp. Thane stood silent for a moment, knowing Victoria MacRath was telling the truth as she believed it.

'When Duncan got back ahead of Peter didn't he notice your car was gone?'

'No.' She shook her head quickly. 'I knew he wouldn't. Usually Duncan leaves his car at the front of the house overnight. He'd just presume mine was in the garage.'

Colin Thane took a slow, deep breath realizing how neatly everything had been accidentally made to order, from the housekeeper being out onward. But it had still depended upon Victoria MacRath.

Mother Bear – as a description, it couldn't have been nearer the mark. He felt something coming close to sympathy for her, but there was still one harsh truth she had to face. Now might be better than later.

'So all both of you had to do was sit back and watch us chase our tails,' he commented. 'Watch us – even when it came to Duncan.'

'I told you I wouldn't have let that happen,' she said wearily. 'I have two sons, Chief Inspector – not one and a half, whatever you may think. Peter and I – well, we both hoped you'd end up believing some casual prowler had killed that girl.'

'The way Peter arranged it?' He faced her stonily. 'Doreen Ashton wasn't killed in any quarrel, Victoria. She was poisoned in cold blood.'

'Poisoned?' She echoed the word in a shattered whisper.

'Peter lied,' nodded Thane. 'We think he got hold of some of his father's old heart medicine – strophanthus. That's what killed her. You had some of it left, hadn't you?'

Her face was all the answer he needed and he turned to go. But her hand caught his arm.

172

'Can you stop Duncan in time?' she asked with a low desperation.

He shrugged. The moth had begun battering its wings against the kerosene lamp as he walked to where Katherine Manson stood waiting.

'Keep an eye on Mrs MacRath,' he said tiredly.

The girl nodded. She wore a fur jacket and looked cold. But he also saw the mixture of fear and anxiety in her eyes.

'We'll get Robby, don't worry.' He twisted a convincing grin and glanced at his watch. Unbelievably, barely five minutes had passed since the Millside car had reached the clearing. 'Waiting is one thing you'll have in common with Mrs MacRath.'

'Her?' The girl frowned. 'I thought –'

He stopped her with a shake of his head and looked back. Victoria MacRath still hadn't moved and her head was erect. But she was looking out into the night again, and tears were streaming down her cheeks.

Slapping the girl encouragingly on the rump, he hurried down to Moss and the circle of rallymen.

The stocky, cheerful man with the torch had it all worked out. His name was MacTavish, he shoved his fur hat back on a bald forehead, and slapped the map he had spread against a rock.

'Who says there's a problem?' he asked his audience with an easy confidence. 'All we need is a little luck.' A forefinger stabbed down on the linen-backed paper. 'These fake pace-notes are planned to knock Duncan off the route near here. So we're talking about a fifty mile distance from the start, right?'

'With no way of stopping him,' declared a pessimist in the group around him. 'I reckon he's more than halfway to where it'll happen by now. Through the first two controls, anyway.'

'Maybe a helicopter might do it,' suggested a bulky figure in a sheepskin jacket.

'Not a chance in these hills by night.' MacTavish shook his head and grinned. 'Try it, and we'll end up looking for the helicopter as well. That's not the way.'

'Then how do we do it?' demanded Phil Moss impatiently. He glanced at Thane, who was standing near him. 'We're wasting time.'

'Here's how.' MacTavish took the rebuke easily and raced his finger over the map. 'That's roughly the Two Hundred route – a damned big oval through the forest, give or take half a million bends. We just cut across the flaming oval, that's all!'

It seemed too simple. Thane pushed forward and peered at the map in the steady torch-beam.

'Can we do it?' he asked.

'The map says yes.' MacTavish nodded positively. 'I'll show you – these lines, Chief Inspector. Forestry work roads, that's all they are. God knows what state they'll be in because they're not meant for the tourist trade. But look where they run and how they link up.' He stood back confidently. 'I reckon a good navigator could plot you a sixteen mile way straight across. You wouldn't just join the rally route – you'd land right where it matters, on that road where the pace-notes should shove him.'

'A good navigator?' Thane considered him thoughtfully. 'You?'

'I always did talk too much.' MacTavish grinned, nodded, and quickly folded his map. 'Who'll be your driver?'

'We've got our own,' said Thane.

'A fuzz-type jockey?' MacTavish blinked at the idea then shrugged. 'Well, we can frighten the hell out of each other, I suppose. You'd better have a back-up car in case things go wrong.'

A minute later they were in the Millside car and on their way, MacTavish up front beside Erickson, Thane and Moss in the rear seat. One of the County cars followed close behind and the other had been left to act as a radio link.

The map folded on his knee, the torch clicking on to light it at brief intervals, MacTavish kept them on the road through the trees for about a mile then told Erickson to turn left on to a narrower track Thane hadn't even noticed ahead.

The surface was broken and rough, the car bounced hard on its springs, and gravel spattered from its wheels as they started a sharp upward climb. Behind them, the headlamps of the County car danced wildly as it followed their lead.

'Watch for a left bend,' warned MacTavish. He grinned approvingly as his bend, a sharp near-hairpin, came up and Erickson sent the car snarling round it. 'All okay in the back, Chief Inspector?'

'We're still here.' Thane grabbed for support as they bucked over a pothole. 'Is it all like this?'

'Mostly.' MacTavish's face sobered for a moment in the shadowed glow of the instrument panel. 'This is the Queen Elizabeth Forest Park – and there's one hell of a lot of trees out there. Spruce, pine and larch if you want to get technical, forty-two thousand acres of the things with the odd mountain to break the monotony.'

A boulder scored the car's underside with a rasping bang and Moss swore as his head hit the roof.

'We wear crash helmets when we're rallying,' said MacTavish. Suiting the words, he took his own from the floor at his feet and put it on in place of the fur hat. 'But I wouldn't worry too much, Inspector – the way I've heard it, all cops have thick skulls.'

175

He turned back to his map before Moss could think of an answer. The way the car was swaying and bouncing, Moss didn't really care anyway.

They lost the County car after five miles. The headlights which had been following them simply disappeared. MacTavish shrugged, muttered possibilities ranging from ditches to outright disaster, and talked Erickson through a tense series of turns and junctions. Two roe deer complicated things halfway through, suddenly appearing in their lights and springing off into the trees at the last instant before the car seemed certain to hit them.

A little later, they broke briefly through the tree-line and were able to increase speed on a stretch of better road blasted straight across a mountainside. Far in the distance, Thane saw car lights moving, and MacTavish saw them too.

'The Two Hundred route,' he said with a grin. 'These boys are probably wondering why so few cars are chasing after them.' Then his mouth tightened briefly. 'We'll make it. Duncan's a friend of mine – and young Robby Deacon's all right too, even if he does have this crazy notion about being tomorrow's super-fuzz.'

The road slipped down the slope again, back into dense, enveloping forest. This time the surface stayed better but there were even more blind bends and corners and MacTavish mumbled an apology about the map's inadequacies. Beside him, Erickson had sweat beading his forehead and sat tight-lipped with strain while he wrestled with the wheel and fought a constant variation between accelerator and gears and brakes – saving seconds at every chance.

But, decided Thane, maybe it was even worse at the

rear. He and Moss could do nothing but sit and trust, and Moss had gone absolutely quiet.

Fifteen of the sixteen miles had clicked past on the instrument panel. They skidded round the edge of a rocky outcrop, with a brief glimpse of a waterfall plunging down into the empty blackness far below. MacTavish licked his lips, checked his map with the torch, and glanced round.

'Almost there.' He forced a parody of his usual grin. 'Either we're ahead of Duncan or – well, if he did crash it wasn't a brew-up job. We'd see the fire by now.'

Erickson put the car hard into another bend. MacTavish shifted to face the front again – then his mouth fell open in alarm as the headlights shone on the projecting trunk of a felled tree.

An instant later the car slammed straight in. The world seemed to erupt in a scream of ripping metal and spraying glass, the lights went out, the engine stalled – then suddenly everything was silent.

Shakily, Thane picked himself up from the floor at the rear. His head had hit the seat in front as he was thrown forward, one hand had been cut by glass, but otherwise he was intact. Moss was struggling up too, cursing and brushing glass from his clothes. Then, at the same time, they realized that Erickson was slumped motionless in his seat-belt behind the wheel and MacTavish, though stirring, was moaning.

They got out. The whole front of the car was embedded deep into the tree, as if it were some giant, blunt harpoon. In the night darkness, the only sounds were the wind, the occasional spit and crackle from the cooling exhaust, and the continued moans from their navigator.

The front passenger door was jammed. Running round to the driver's side, Thane got that door open, unclipped Erickson's seat belt and with Moss's help dragged the big man out on to the road. Then they went back for MacTavish.

MacTavish looked up at them and grimaced. He'd already freed his belt but gave a stifled cry of pain as Thane tried to move him.

'Easy –' he appealed through clenched teeth – 'my legs.'

By some miracle he still had the torch in his hand and it worked. He shone it down and they saw for themselves. The impact had split the car's bulkhead and he was trapped just below the knees.

'You'll need a – a bloody rescue squad to get me out,' said MacTavish flatly, switching off the torch. 'How's Erickson?'

'Coming round,' answered Moss over Thane's shoulder. He went back to where Erickson lay, checked again, and returned. 'He'll do. Like you said, all cops have thick heads.'

'Good.' MacTavish licked his lips and glanced at Thane. 'Of all the damnable luck –'

'How far to go?' asked Thane tensely.

'Not much more than – than half a mile.' MacTavish read his thoughts and nodded. 'You might make it.'

'Yes.' Thane glanced back at Erickson. Moss had dragged him into a sitting position against a tree and had his head down between his knees. 'What about you?'

MacTavish sniffed the air hard. 'The fuel tank's all right – no worries. Switch off the ignition and that'll do it.'

Quickly, Thane switched off and drew out the key.

'Good.' Grimacing a smile, MacTavish handed him the torch. 'On your way.'

Erickson was still totally dazed and had blood from a head cut covering most of his face. But he managed a nod and a mumble when Thane spoke to him.

178

Then, together, the torch-beam lighting their way, Thane and Moss started off down the track at a fast trot. Twigs snapped under their feet, fallen branches tried to trip them and almost every other step offered a pothole or an ankle-jarring boulder.

Swearing at first, then silent and sweating, breathing more and more heavily, they kept on through the eerie tunnel of trees. An unseen bird rose with a cry and a beating of wings which brought a rain of leaves and pine-cones down around them. Other creatures stirred and rustled – but all that mattered was the few yards shown by the torch, the ribbon of track that still stretched on.

They'd been going for five minutes when they heard the car. A distant glow of light showed ahead, it came nearer with the engine louder by the moment – and suddenly became a crazy, tortured squeal of tyres.

They came to a despairing halt as the squeal ended in a crash which echoed through the night. The car's lights vanished. For a moment longer they heard a grating rumble punctuated by sharp cracks like pistol-shots. Then, once again, there was only the sound of the wind and their own laboured breathing.

Together, they started running again with a new desperation. But only five hundred yards on, as they rounded a bend, Moss gasped incoherently and grabbed Thane's arm, pulling him to a halt. He pointed along the track, unable to speak.

Thane steadied the torch, and clicked it off quickly. Peter MacRath's grey Jaguar coupé lay parked neatly and empty under the trees a stone's throw ahead. Hurrying forward, he shone the torch for a moment through the driver's window and saw the key still in the ignition.

Reaching him, face lined with strain, Moss clutched the car for support and stood panting.

'Damn him,' Moss managed. 'He – he wanted to make sure, didn't he?'

'Come on.' Thane started off again, forcing a new effort from his protesting lungs and muscles though he would have given most things to rest for just a moment longer.

But he couldn't, he daren't.

Two hundred yards on, at a sharper bend in the track, they reached the spot where the other car had crashed. Broken glass littered the edge of the track at the start of a wide, raw gap torn through the young trees which formed the verge. But beyond that was a savage, bare downhill slope of gravelled scree and rock, a slope now with a great sliding scar carved across it. Even the weak moonlight which filtered through a cloud showed the way it was littered with broken branches and debris.

At the bottom, where tall, thick pines began again, lay the upturned wreckage of Duncan MacRath's rally Ford. Thane used the torch – then sprang forward as it showed two figures struggling on the ground beside the wreck. One was Peter MacRath, with what looked like a heavy tyre-lever in his hand. The other man wore rally overalls and a crash helmet.

Shouting, Thane went down the scree slope in a wild, running, jumping rush. Below, MacRath smashed the tyre-lever down again and his opponent fell limp. For a moment Peter MacRath stared up the slope then he began running for the trees.

He vanished among them as Thane and Moss reached the car. Quickly, Thane stooped beside the figure on the ground as the man made a feeble effort to rise.

It was Robby Deacon. As Thane's hand touched him the lanky youngster jerked and threw up an arm in a feeble attempt to fight again.

'Easy, boy.' Thane grabbed him by the wrist. 'It's all right. Where's Duncan?'

For a moment, Deacon stared at his face unbelievingly then with an expression of relief jerked his head towards the car. 'Still inside. He – he's alive, but smashed up. I was –' he moved and gave a grunt of pain – 'I was trying to get him out when that maniac arrived.'

'Phil.' Thane nodded to Moss, who scrambled for the car.

'Sir –' Deacon forced himself upright a little. 'Those pace-notes went crazy –'

'We know.' Thane got to his feet and saw Moss working inside the car. 'I'll be back.'

He turned away and ran for the trees where Peter MacRath had vanished.

A hundred yards in among the pines and Colin Thane was left feeling he might have travelled a hundred miles. Everything in the outside world was shut off and lost amongst the forest and its overhead interlace of branches. Every step he took, his feet crackled on twigs and dried leaves and all the swinging torch-beam could show was a waiting, apparently never-ending maze of trees.

But when he stopped, a steady, crashing noise reached his ears from not too far ahead. Taking a deep breath, he plunged on again in pursuit and ignored the low branches which clawed and whipped at his face.

Gradually, the crashing ahead became louder as he closed on the running man. The torch beam caught Peter MacRath for an instant before he disappeared between two trees.

Suddenly, the crashing stopped. Slowing, Thane moved forward cautiously with the torch beam probing from side to side – but when MacRath made his move it was from behind, with the tyre-lever swinging.

The sharp crackle of twigs brought Thane round in time. He managed to catch the tyre-lever's downward swing on the torch then, as the torch smashed with the impact, he went for MacRath in a twisting sideways tackle.

They went down as the metal bar hit him a glancing blow on the shoulder. His whole arm went numb but he rolled over on the twigs, still grappling MacRath, and the next blow crashed uselessly into the ground.

Thane slammed his fist into the man's face, heard MacRath grunt with pain, then rolled again and pinned the tyre-lever to the ground with his body. Cursing, MacRath tried to free it – and Thane grabbed the man's other wrist with its adhesive strapping and twisted hard.

This time MacRath screamed his agony, abandoned the tyre-lever and tore himself free. Scrambling to his feet he began running again with Thane close behind him.

Through the near absolute darkness, cannoning off trees, tripping, stumbling, pursued and pursuer kept stubbornly on. Vaguely, Thane realized they were heading back the way he had come – then the edge of the trees was ahead and he broke through into faint moonlight again to see MacRath maybe ten yards ahead and scrambling up the scree slope towards the road.

Thane felt exhausted. Every breath had become an agony and a strange, growing bellowing roar was in his ears. But he forced himself on, tackling the sliding rise while stones and gravel kicked down by MacRath showered around him. All he could think of was that if MacRath got back to his car it still wouldn't be over.

He began to see through a reddening haze. The bellowing roar in his ears was becoming louder as he lurched and clawed upward. Above him, he was aware MacRath had reached the top. The man started to run – then froze, bathed in light.

Brakes screeched and almost drowned MacRath's scream. There was a bang – and something like a broken rag doll was thrown through the air and down on to the slope. It rolled to the bottom and lay still.

The bellowing roar was still there, but with an irregular, idling note. Bewildered, Thane clawed up the last few feet, heard doors open and close and excited voices – then saw and understood.

It was the County car, the one they'd lost behind them far back on the dash over the forestry tracks. Only one headlamp was working, its bodywork was gashed and scraped, and the broken silencer pipe hung loose while the engine continued its full-throated bellow.

A moment later someone had the sense to switch the ignition off. The County sergeant and two men in rally clothes had reached him by then and a constable was coming to join them, carrying a heavy battery lantern.

'I didn't have a chance, sir,' said the County sergeant in a shaken voice. 'I tried to brake, but I didn't have a chance –'

Thane could only stand and gulp air for a full minute. Then he nodded and forced a grin.

'What kept you?' he asked weakly.

'We went straight into the biggest bloody ditch in the world.' The County man snatched the lantern, switched it on, and played its powerful beam down the slope. He stopped it at the limp form below and moistened his lips. 'Who is it, Chief Inspector?'

'Peter MacRath.' Thane fumbled for a cigarette, got it between his lips, and someone struck a match for him. He took two long draws, the smoke rasping his lungs 'I'll cope here. Duncan MacRath's car is further along – you're needed there.'

One of the men gave him a hand-torch and then they hurried off, the big battery lamp playing on the ground ahead of them. In a moment Thane heard shouts and they started sliding their way down towards the wrecked car. He took a last draw on the cigarette, tossed it aside, and made his own slow way down to Peter MacRath.

The fair-haired man was lying in a twisted huddle at the bottom of the slope. He was conscious and watched the approaching torch-beam sardonically. Blood oozed from his mouth and his slow, rasping breath told its own story.

'If you've come to – to hold my hand, don't bother,' he said hoarsely and bitterly as Thane knelt beside him. 'I can – can do without that privilege, damn you.'

The effort brought on a racking cough which left him with more blood bubbling out from between his lips.

'Lie still,' said Thane quietly. 'They're getting Duncan free from the car – then they'll be along to help here.'

'Why bother?' MacRath gave a grimacing shake of his head. 'I – hell, I always did back losers. Though this one – it worked while it lasted.'

'We know,' Thane told him. 'Most of it, anyway.'

'Doreen Ashton.' The dead girl's name came from MacRath like a feeble curse. He lay silent for a moment, breathing in those rasping, agonized gasps. 'You know about the receipts?'

'Yes,' nodded Thane. 'How did she find out?'

'It was when – when that damned lawyer began howling. I – I told her it was a misunderstanding, that I'd handle it on my own. I didn't know she'd dug out

184

the file.' MacRath coughed and closed his eyes briefly while his face contorted with fresh pain. 'Her initials were on – on the receipt references except she – she knew she hadn't typed them. Too damned efficient – that was her trouble.'

'So you poisoned her,' said Thane softly. 'Tell me about it.'

'Now?' The bright eyes seemed to mock him. 'Why not? I met her – talked her into going back to the office. Then I tried to – tell her she had it wrong. I said it – it was maybe Duncan and she came round a little. But I saw it wasn't going to work for long and there – well, I just had to silence her. So I said right, have a drink.'

'You were going to kill her from the start or you wouldn't have had that stuff along,' said Thane grimly. He used his handkerchief to wipe away more of the blood oozing from the man's lips. 'That's how it really was, MacRath. Why lie?'

'So you're right.' MacRath managed a shrug. 'Whisky, Thane – they don't taste it in whisky. Got that tip from my old man.'

'Then you let her die, you got her down to the car, and took her back to Leyland Street,' summarized Thane tiredly. 'We know the next part. But why did you try to kill Duncan? Had he found out something?'

'No.' MacRath's voice was weaker and his rasping breathing was slowing. 'But – but he would, some-time. Or Victoria would go soft. I – when I hurt my wrist, I got the idea.' He twisted a weak grin. 'Knock Duncan off, make it – make it look like a rally acci-dent. Hard luck, Duncan. You – you made a mistake in your own damned pace-notes.'

'Then you'd be left running the firm, you could cover up what you wanted.' Thane nodded his under-standing. 'But that would still leave your mother.'

'She'd never talk.' MacRath mumbled the words. 'She'd –' He stopped, stared at Thane, and fought down a cough. 'Did she – damn you, did she?'

Thane looked at him impassively and said nothing.

'The stupid old bitch,' forced MacRath. 'I –' He broke off into another blood-bubbling cough. It ended in a sighing rasp and his head fell limp, the bright eyes staring blindly at the torch-beam.

Colin Thane looked at him for a moment longer, then switched off the torch, got to his feet, and started walking towards the bright glare of the battery lantern.

More cars and a Range-Rover ambulance arrived within the next half-hour. There was a doctor with the ambulance and he already had one patient. It was MacTavish, who sat up and grinned as Duncan MacRath was loaded aboard on a stretcher.

'You look fine, boy,' he declared. 'Think of all those nurses they've got stacked up waiting for us.'

Duncan MacRath managed to twitch a feeble hand in greeting. His other hand was tight in the grip of Victoria MacRath, who had bullied and cajoled her way over in one of the Range-Rover's jump seats. Her eyes were still swollen and red, and she'd spent five long minutes standing at the foot of the scree slope beside the blanket-covered body which still lay there.

'Watch how you handle that stretcher,' she snapped at the men loading it aboard. 'My son is –' She stopped short, then realized they were watching her. 'My son needs proper care and I'm here to make sure he gets it,' she finished with a defiant pride.

Thane watched until the ambulance doors were closed then turned away. Erickson and young Robby Deacon were sitting on the grass at the edge of the track, both sporting bandages and with the bunch of young rookie cops from the Training Centre listening to their every word. They'd come over in another car somehow, and Kate Manson had been with them. She sat closest to Deacon, and Deacon had his arm casually around her shoulders.

He twisted a grin at the sight and walked down towards the battered County car which was drawn off the road and being used as a radio link. Phil Moss was at its opened door, using the microphone, and he beckoned as he saw Thane.

'Stand by, sir,' he said into the microphone. 'He's here now.' Then he quickly passed it to Thane. 'Buddha Ilford wants to talk to you. I've told him the score.'

'Thane?' The city C.I.D. chief's voice boomed over the static crackle from the car speaker. 'Can you hear me? Over.'

Ilford trusted radio even less than he did telephones. Grimacing, Thane pressed the 'Send' button.

'Loud and very clear,' he acknowledged briefly.

'Good. Moss says it's all buttoned up.' Ilford sounded relaxed and cheerful. 'From what I can make out, none of the – ah – other investors should suffer and I've a feeling the MacRaths can sort out the losses in time. Over.'

'I think they'll try,' agreed Thane woodenly.

'So we're lucky all round, eh?' crackled Ilford's voice. 'Nobody too badly hurt at your end, if we don't count Peter MacRath. And I wouldn't. Over.'

'The ambulance has just started back,' Thane told him. 'Mrs MacRath is aboard if you want to meet it at the hospital.'

'I will. But no charges, eh? And – ah – don't worry about that duty car you wrote off. Over.'

'I wasn't going to anyway,' said Thane grimly.

187

'No.' Ilford's voice faded for a moment under the static then came back stronger. 'Still there, Thane? Over.'

'Still here.' Thane heard Moss give an amused belch at his side and scowled at the microphone.

'Good. One last little problem for you,' said Ilford airily. 'Remember your four Spaniards? They're back in the cells at Millside – but eight of them this time. Same riot, same reason, same charges. Sort it out, will you. Over.'

Thane released the 'Send' button and swore incredulously.

'Tell him to get stuffed,' suggested Moss, grinning. 'That doctor dropped off a bottle of single-malt – and I know where that damned County sergeant hid it.'

The car speaker came to life again, Ilford's voice demanding an answer. Thane tossed the microphone on to the driving seat and firmly closed the car door.

'Radio reception gets hellish in these hills,' he said mildly. 'Where's that bottle, Phil?'

And they walked away.